LOFOTEN-
 RUDI

Scenes of a Sailor's life

Short stories of a naval officer and

**Sailing instructor as a Skipper
of yachts**

Rudolf Neumann

Bibliographic information of the German National Library

The German National Library records this publication in the Deutsche Nationalbibliographie. Detailed bibliographic data are available on the Internet at http://dnb.dnb.de

© 2018 Rudolf Neumann
All rights reserved
Production and publishing:
BoD - Books on Demand, Norderstedt
Contact: Lofotenrudi@freenet.de
Originally published under the titel
„Lofoten-Rudi, Szenen eines Seglerlebens, 2018"
Translated by Rudolf Neumann & Dave Hughes
Cover picture: Marlies Schaper, watercolor
Cover design, layout, editing: Clemens Rettberg

ISBN: 9783746074511

About the book

260,000 nautical miles of sailing: North Sea, Baltic Sea, Mediterranean, Black Sea, North Atlantic, Caribbean and Pacific.

In more than 40 sailing short stories Rudolf Neumann, called Lofoten-Rudi, takes us along on his trips, into a world full of sailing adventures and curious events.

A work that is always entertaining, often exciting and which is sure to invoke many smiles. Not just for sailors, but also for those who just want to get a taste of sailing life.

Contents

The Nickname Lofoten-Rudi

In 1978, rarely would someone have thought of sailing with a 10m yacht, with no heating, from Hamburg, far to the north, beyond the polar circle.

At this time, there was neither GPS nor DECCA or SAT-Nav. And the good thermal clothing was not on the market.

With my S & S 34 called "SUNRISE" I nevertheless decided to take a trip to the Lofoten Islands.

On board was my fellow sailor Bernd Gallbach, usually called Galle.

The first part of the trip past Denmark and southern Norway went without major problems. We celebrated Midsummer Night on the island of Ona. Further north still we sailed into a violent north-westerly storm, with heavy gales.

Galle later described the waves as being as high as a two storey house.

In this storm, one of our foresails suffered severe damage and would need repair later back in Wedel at "Brother Sail".

We finally reached the port of Svolvaer in the Lofoten.

On the way back we wanted to sail to the Faroe Islands, but again we ran into heavy weather which damaged the mast wedges and we had to turn off before reaching the islands. We returned via Lerwick on the Shetlands and the English east coast to our home town Wedel in Holstein.

This was the summary of the trip.

I took the damaged foresail to the sailmaker for repair and returned to collect it when completed. The sailmaker clearly had not noticed the proper name of his client, and hanging on the sail bag was a label with the inscription "LOFOTEN-RUDI".

The nickname was born and has remained ever-since.

It was the truth

In 1979, as Captain-Lieutenant and sailing Officer of a squadron of the German Navy, I had the task of carrying out a navigation instruction and training exercise with the masters (Chiefs) of the squadron from Borkum to Edinburgh. A sailing yacht of the type 7 KR (keel weighted Racing Cruiser) with the name "Monsun" was made available to us.

At that time the squadron had just signed on a new staff physician.

Doctors were in short supply from the medical faculty. They wore the blue uniform of the Navy, but they usually had no idea of the sea, the Navy, and certainly not of yachts or sails.

In order to compensate for his lack of knowledge, the doctor wanted to participate in this trip.

I was against it at first, but then decided to take him with me because a doctor on board could be useful.

In those days the 7 KR ships had a wet room with a pump-toilet and a spacious pull-out washbasin, which, however did not stand out particularly from the wooden panel and was not immediately recognizable.

The journey went without problems at first. The doctor, however, did not fit in with the crew because of his allegedly higher level of education.

It happened that one of the masters appeared on the stairs from the cockpit into the lower deck area with a wet head and hair. "Our doctor's spontaneous question:" Where did you wash yourself?

He received the short answer: "The toilet!" Instead of asking more closely the doctor remained silent.

After a short time someone else came back with wet hair.

Again the doctor asked: "Where have you washed?" And was answered: "the toilet!"

Afterwards, the doctor dived into the wet room to check it out but did not come upon the secret.

Later as people were getting wet again, the Doc suddenly asked me: "Lieutenantcommander, Sir is it true that people wash themselves in the toilet?"

I answered: "Of course, where else?"

Until the end of the trip, the doctor washed in a plastic bowl on the aft ship.

The Court Martial

In the days when the Federal Republic of Germany was still wealthy it could afford to have a larger army, and similarly also a larger navy. Within this it also maintained several sailing yachts for training purposes in various locations.

These yachts were also used during internal and external sailing regattas.

It was on one of these regattas that I participated as a shipsmaster of a 6.5 KR. yacht called "Magellan".

The fleet was headed by a 7 KR. yacht commanded by a well known, but not very popular, Frigate Captain. He had a pithy growling voice, and was of absolutely impeccable appearance with a dust-free and spotless uniform, as well as special trademark gleaming white gloves when on the tiller.

In the course of the race, our fleet fell into a sudden fog wall with very light winds.

After a while, nobody knew whereabouts they were within the fleet of boats nor where any of the competition were. Suddenly, a loud booming voice sounded in front of us through the fog wall. "If the spinnaker starts flapping again, I will have you court martialed."

Then we knew at once, in front of us lay the KR7 of the said frigate captain.

The subsequent victory of the regatta then made the "court martial" superfluous.

Also Customs Officiers can be controlled

On a voyage with a service sailing yacht from Kiel to Granton Harbor / Edinburgh, I was the Lieutenantcommander in charge.

Because it was more convenient, the whole crew (six men) did not wear uniforms, but civilian shirts and jeans.

The journey went without incident. After arriving in Granton we awaited the authorities, that is, Harbourmaster and Customs.

After about two hours, just at low water, an irrate Customs officer appeared, in a blue trousers and a white shirt, along with a trainee officer high up on the pier. He was obviously stressed.

The climbing ladder leading to us was oily and very slippery, so that both uniforms suffered accordingly. When both reached the deck of the ship, he vented his anger. He spat out brief questions: "Strong spirits ..., how many bottles ..., cigarettes ..., tobacco ..., and coffee" etc.

Order to the trainee officer "All needs to be sealed in a locker"

I quietly objected: "When we are dealing with warships of Her British Majesty, Eg in the "Kieler Woche", it is completely different, since nothing needs to be sealed.

He answered: "Warships operating under Queens's regulations continue to operate under different rules".

Then I: "Alright Sir: This is a naval ship as well, it belongs to the German Federal Navy and I am Lieutenantcommander Neumann, commanding officer of this warship.

He questioned: "Can you prove that?"

I answered: "Of course Sir, here is my I. D. Card."

After that, he gave in completely and simply said, "Sir, excuse me sir, sir nothing has to be sealed impounded!"

"I'm going off board", repeating several times "sir, excuse me sir."

By now I was back on track. "Now show me to the nearest telegraph office so I can communicate with the fleet."

He did so most diligently.

Hard Ironmen

In the 1950s I sailed on a naval cadet training ship whose homeport was Kiel. Our first watch officer was a swimming fanatic, and would swim no matter what the temperature of the water.

He simply set a temperature limit, above which would still swim. Usually it was seven degrees. Above this there was a need to swim.

The temperature measurement recorded on the bridge of the ship often resulted in 7.2 ° or 7.3 °, which is above the lower limit, even in November / December with a cutting east wind blowing across the ice cold Baltic Sea.

A few years later, on a sailing trip to the Lofoten Islands, with my S & S 34 "Sunrise", the remains of a fishing net got caught up on the propeller when moored in the port of Svolvaer. The engine stopped immediately. Out of gear, she ran perfectly, so something had to be blocking the ship's propeller. A dive was therefore required. Temperature of the water was a creepy 6 °. So a swimsuit was called for, onto the pier telling yourself you were warm, then jump into the ice cold water. At first one was paralyzed and could not move. After overcoming the freezing paralysis, with a knife gripped between the teeth, one had to swim under the water to reach the propeller shaft and free it from the tangled fishing net.

It was not easy, because the plastic netting was completely melted by the friction with the shaft.

In total there were four dives by the skipper and three dives from "Galle", then everything was free again. The engine system finally returned to business.

This meant, after some rum grog and use of all the available blankets, a night shivering to overcome the cold. Problem solved, everything again normal!

Many years later, I was now 70 years old, I was commissioned to transfer the 35 m long Wishbone ketch "Sintra" from Boothbay Harbor (Main USA) to Glückstadt on the Elbe.

At this time of the year, it was March, it was still winter in Boothbay, and there were still snowfalls and huge snowdrifts on the pier. Just beyond the ship ice was present at the sides of the river. Further up river the ships were still frozen in. The water temperature was about two degrees. The Sintra had not moved in a long time, so I could see in the clear water that the propeller was completely covered with sea weed and mussels. The propulsion efficiency was going to be zero.

I wondered where a diver could be reached for cleaning the screw. That was settled quickly because I found I had a crewmember from Cuxhaven on board, a trained guy with strength and endurance. He said, "We'll be away in no time."

He appeared in a bathing suit on the deck, ran about to get warm then jumped into the water with scrubbing brush and scraper. He stayed in the water and scrubbed the propeller clean, then emerged, ran about again to get warm. So within half an hour everything was sorted.

Such Ironmen are sometimes needed!

Blind in one eye

My Sunrise was in Glückstadt's Yacht works. I was working on the underside of the boat, which had been painted with hard antifouling. Whilst doing this a splitter must have fallen into my left eye during grinding. I had not noticed it. On the way back to Hamburg the eye was very red, aching and I also got a headache. Probably a normal conjunctivitis, I thought, and that evening at home I put in a few eye drops.

The next day I was on holiday and was due to take Ulli Hübner from Schilksee and guests, known as "The Happy Four", for a Gin Fizz, on a trip across the Baltic Sea to Samsö and back.

The morning came, it was a Sunday, the eye was not any better, but my girlfriend and I drove to Schilksee.

In the office of the charter company, my inflamed red eye was spotted immediately, but I said, "With a few eyedrops, it will pass."

The eye did not get any better, but as long as the cool wind blew in, it was tolerable

In Ballen on Samsö I went to my bunk in the evening. The eye burned and hurt, so I put in drops once again. When I woke up in the morning, it was already daylight, the yellow sunlight filtering through the deck appeared to me as a diffuse brownish light.

I closed the sick eye and saw the yellow sunlight crystal clear, then I closed the healthy eye and saw nothing.

I was instantly awake. Now something had to be done immediately. No doctor in Ballen so what to do?

Since I was in the active Navy service, I called to my colleagues over Lyngby-Radio (a coastal service in Denmark) with a request for help from the Rescue Coordination Centre-Glücksburg. They said if necessary they would organise emergency help by helicopter.

After a short while I again spoke to Lyngby radio and the „Flag officer Denmark" in Denmark was on the line. I got the order to go to Tuno immediately, as everything was prepared.

So we cast off and set off to Tuno.

Already waiting at the mooring we saw the harbour master, who had ridden down on his bicycle along with his dog. "Very important Commander," he said.

My girlfriend and I followed him, believing he would lead us to a doctor, but we ended up at the house of the midwife.

The lady immediately began an investigation as follows: "Sit down in the chair!"

Then she moved a pointer, which I was to follow. "Look here, Look there, Can you see?" (Nothing was to be seen.)

No, nothing in one eye.

"Oh, that's bad, quite bad, you must see the doctor."

That's what I wanted too.

She telephoned the mainland, the eye doctor was not there.

"Must go to Hov, then Clinic Arhus."

OK. The harbour master was equally understanding and arranged a fishing cutter Naval reserve to Hov, then a taxi to the eye clinic at Arhus. I was straight there.

Three young ophthalmologists, examining me using a slit lamp: "We'll get it sorted."

I was given an ointment to put in my eye. Use it regularly then everything would be OK. Getting it rechecked by an ophthalmologist was an option but not absolutely necessary.

We went back to Schilksee and reached the home port, then we drove straight to Hamburg.

Afterwards I called into the German Federal Armed Forces hospital (at that time still a hospital) it was again Sunday, a superintendant of the eye department spoke to me and said that there was no ophthalmologist at the weekend, but in urgent cases he could call one by pager.

He did just that and my girlfriend drove me to the Bundeswehr hospital.

It was the head physician who put me in front of the slit lamp. His diagnosis: The iris is totally glued and is no longer mobile, we will certainly try everything to cure it.

I was immediately admitted to hospital and started therapy. Day and night, rinse, ointment, rinse, ointment, etc. After a week, the eye worked again and I was released. Thank God!

Record Run in Winter

In February 1982, we were at the management academy of the German armed forces stationed in Hamburg, the idea arose to try to sail to Oslo in the shortest possible time, in winter temperatures, using a service sailing yacht.

At the naval school in Flensburg-Murwik we were given a service sailing yacht of the type HANSEAT 70 B with the name "SMARAGD (Emerald)".

The crew consisted of five non-commissioned officers as well as myself, a Lieutenantcommander, as a skipper.

The equipping of the boat went quickly and smoothly and so we left Mürwik on a cold winter day at 10.00.

We had quickly left the fjord with favorable winds, and now under full sail at North-West 5-6, we reached the Great Belt strait in Denmark.

The night was clear and cold but we made good progress. The wind blew strong and at the watch was replaced after two hours guard.

Navigationally there were no problems, it was on a clear night and warning beacons were clearly visible.

Already shortly after midnight we had passed KORSÖR port with its strong ferry traffic and by daybreak were already in the southern Kattegat.

Over the course of the day, temperatures rose to just below freezing point, often leading to snow showers with correspondingly gusty winds.

Before we reached the tip of Läsö Island, the wind turned to the north and we were again in some snow showers. In poor visibility, we had to make two cross tacks.

As we proceeded the wind veered back by two compass points, and the journey continued steadily.

In the meantime, we sailed at high speed through the Skagerrak and, shortly before daybreak, we could see in the distance the light beacon on Färder Island at the entrance of the Oslo fjord, just above the horizon.

We reached the Oslo fjord and came upon a winter panorama.

The landscape was still deep in snow, and thick icicles were hanging down from the rock walls where water had once flowed.

Shortly behind the Dröbak narrow, the wind, which had blown us so far, dropped and we had to use the engine to take us to the port of Oslo.

We had taken 52 hours for the 300 nautical miles (with cross tacks). This corresponded to an average speed of 5.76 knots. For a ship of this size, in winter conditions a strong performance.

A berth was found quickly, because the sportsailing was very quiet at this time of year.

Everywhere was still high snow and all the ports showers were unfortunately closed leaving only a public toilet with a small sink to assist us.

We got along as best we could, and the following day had the great fortune that a german fast patrol boat squadron and Tender entered into the harbour.

We immediately stopped and went along to one of the boats.

The cleaning problems were solved at a stroke. With our comrades on the Tender we had plenty of hot water for showers and washing before going sight seeing in the town, all before setting off on the journey home. After getting back and returning the boat to the naval school in Flensburg Murwik, our trip was correspondingly honored.

In the boat house at the school, there was a board on which the data from our expedition was recorded.

„Too Hot to Bathe"

In 1979 my friend (Galle) Bernd Gallbach and I sailed my "Sunrise", an S & S 34, from Hamburg for five weeks around Iceland, we also made station in Reykjavik.

Because of the long journey we were completely encrusted. At the time smaller yachts did not have rear showers with hot and cold water. In addition, we had only 30 liters of fresh water on board, which was used for cooking and drinking water.

After mooring up we went to search for a shower with sponge bag in hand.

There was nothing to find in the vicinity of the harbour. But suddenly a car stopped beside us, the window was cranked down and a nice man asked us in English "Where are you headed?"

"We are looking for a shower!"

"I am a member of the Icelandic life-boat association. I know DGzRS in Bremen. OK. Step in, I will give you a lift to the pool. "

Our objection that we had not exchanged any Icelandic money and had no swimming trunks, did not bother him, and we set off. When we arrived, he obtained tickets for us and some rental bathing trunks. Then he wished us a lot of fun and disappeared.

The poolroom consisted of a 25 m pool, and to the left and right of it were large stone baths in the floor, with steam coming from them all. They had different temperatures.

"Where do we start?"

In one of the pools there were a lot of older people.

"Let us start there, it can not be anything too extraordinary!"

We jumped in! - Oh, fright, the water was boiling hot.

To keep "face", we stayed in for 5-6 minutes, then we leapt, crimson with "first degree" burns, into the large swimming pool.

Conclusion: Even the best plans sometimes backfire.

According to Lenin: "Trust is good, control is better."

The Secret Shower

Many years ago, I was supposed to bring two charter yachts, which were in disarray with transfer passengers, from Málaga to the Canary Islands.

The yachts were two of a kind, ketch-struck ships, originally sailing from Mallorca but running into a thunderstorm, for which the two student skippers from Berlin were obviously no match. After arriving at the port of Malaga, one of the two skippers had immediately taken flight and had departed.

I arrived from Hamburg at midnight in the harbour, found the ships, but there was no one on board. After a short time, the guests and the second skipper came in from the town and I was able to start my questioning. What had happened in the storm? How were the stocks of food, diesel, water, etc.

I realized that nothing was sorted for such a trip.

Most minor repairs I could do myself but for the defective UHF radio I needed a professional to come out the next day.

For the bunk allocation the following day, I divided the crew as I saw necessary. Two homosexuals, who expressed their inclination, obviously did not agree with my way Skippering, and so grabbed their belongings, and left the ship in the night to go to find a hotel.

OK.

The following day everything went according to plan. Since I had the task of leading both yachts, I arranged for the other skipper to remain close to me and and to have the UHF radio - ours was now repaired – always switched on.

After taking on board new supplies we set off to pass through the Strait of Gibraltar. Vessels of this type were only equipped with 200 litres of fresh water, more capacity was not available. This had to meet the needs of both cooking and washing.

As the journey would be long, I arranged for safety reasons not to use the freshwater shower in the foredeck. Showers on deck with brush and seawater would be possible at any time.

Meanwhile we sailed down the African west coast.

I had my bunk in the navigation section on the starboard side of the ship. Above the bunk was the control panel with all the instruments and switches.

One night, I was about to sleep, suddenly the fresh water pressure pump ran in the otherwise quiet ship.

There is someone taking a secret shower. The door to the foreship was closed.

Now I had to make an example. I waited until the sound of the pump fell silent. "Now he's fully soaped up" I thought.

When the pump kicked in again, so they could rinse off the soap, I turned the power switch above me from on to off. The sound of the pump stopped instantly.

The foreship door swung open, and a soapy figure stood in the doorway, and cursed in the Saxon dialect: "Where is the water up front."

I had caught the clandestine shower taker.

I said to them "Outside on the deck is the brush and abundant sea water to rinse."

Secret showering did not occur again for the rest of the trip.

Two days later we fell into a severe sirocco storm. We were well prepared, but due to the terrible visibility in the sandstorm the second ship was lost from the sight and veered out of UHF range.

After the storm subsided I managed, however, with the help of a freight ship with a higher antenna, to bring both ships back together and bring us safely to the port of Arrecife on Lanzarote. After that, we reached our final destination of Puerto Rico on Gran Canaria all on time.

Mission completed!

Mice on the Jutta, Rat on the Libeccio

In 1988, I took over the wooden 20 m Yawl "Jutta" as Skipper and instructor for the DHH (German High Seas Sports Association Hansa) on Elba.

The first trip went from Portoferraio (Elba) around Corsica.

On the Jutta, the galley was in the anterior third of the ship, on the port side just behind the stairs to the lower deck. Behind it came the salon and then, slightly elevated, the very spacious owner's chamber, which was equipped with two opposite berths. I slept in this chamber on the starboard side. During the night, I was awakened by the sounds of light tapping coming from above me, from the beam clamp.

By day, however, nothing was to be found.

On the floor boards in the galley on occasion a few tortellini were seen scattered around. Those sleeping up front had heard the fall of these bits of pasta from the cupboards during the night. After checking we also discovered holes in the cellophane bags in the cupboards. This went on for several nights. It could only be mice.

So, buy mouse trap, put bait on it and in the evening place it in the galley.

Later when we came back on board, terrible squeaking could be heard and as we soon discovered, an adult male mouse was caught in the trap, but he was only caught by the tail and was pulling the trap behind him. He had to be disposed of.

The Tortellini, however, still clicked to the ground on the following nights, and all resetting of the mousetrap was unsuccessful. The other mice were warned. A new method was needed. A glue trap was the solution. It was installed before we next went ashore.

When we came back, the mother mouse and four young mice were caught by it.

We discovered the mice nest a few days later under the refrigerator. It was in the insulating wool, and still contained a good pound of different pasta pieces, a stockpile left by the recently disposed mice.

The mice on the Jutta were thus eliminated.

A year later I got a new ship on Elba, a Gib Sea 442 named Libeccio.

The season of the summer of '89 was over, but the sailors were not yet allowed to go home, because nautical maintenance had yet to be completed.

It was autumn and the Mistral ruled. There was a storm and the rain poured down, everywhere was deserted. I lay alone on the ship in my bunk in the aft starbord cabin. The rain was drumming on the deck, I woke up during the night and suddenly saw in the pale light, from the lamps on the pier, shinning through the porthole, a rat right in front of my face, which was cleaning itself. I was instantly awake, jumped up, and slammed shut the open cabin door, hoping to trap the rat.

Unfortunately, it was not to be.

Over the next few days, I thought the rat would have left the boat, but every now and then, in various bins, I found paper and chewed up cardboard.

A glue trap had to be made.

The glue was prepared and applied to a piece of cardboard, then baited. The cardboard was fastened down with tape, otherwise, if the rat walks with it, the whole ship gets messed up with glue.

The next morning came, the rat was stuck with his feet firmly in the glue. A quick disposal and once again the Libeccio was free of rats!

Midsummernight in Visby and the Flag with the „Werkzeug" (Tools)

The Hartenberg sailing school in Laboe had in its program a 14-day trip to Gotland for midsummer night. The participants should bring along white dress uniform for this occasion.

I was the captain of this trip on a Bavaria 38 with the name "Andoge". The departure day had been set for 19 June 1989, 3 days before midsummer. At a distance of 350 NM this was likely to be a big problem. Hartenberg told me at the departure: "Sail as far as you can, if all goes well. Then try on the return leg to call in at Rügen, then still DDR (East Germany). "He gave me an East German flag, black, red, gold with the symbol of a hammer and circle.

So we set off and reached Gedser on the first evening with a favorable wind. The crew wanted to go in but I remembered the saying of an old pilot at the island Utsira who said: "Rudi, when the winds blow you have to go, otherwise you can stay," and since the wind was favorable I persuaded the crew to continue.

On the following evening, we were already facing Öland's Södra Udde and the wind was blowing vigorously from the right angle.

Once again I convinced everyone to hold out and so we had Gotland in view the next morning and by afternoon arrived ontime for the Midsummer Night in Visby. The white dress uniforms could be used.

Because of the fast journey out we had time to spare on the way back. We sailed through the Kal-marSound to Kalmar, then to Karlskrona, further on to Rönne on Bornholm with a detour to Christiansö, and finally to reach the homeport of Laboe headed in to Saßnitz on the island Rügen.

It was the period of upheaval in the DDR and so for us a level of insecurity.

In the then 12-mile zone, we first met a boat of the DDR's fishery inspectorate. I asked via the VHF radio: "Can we go to Saßnitz as a Western-German yacht?"

Answer: "We do not know, ask Rügen-Radio."

I called Rügen radio and repeated my question.

Answer: "We do not know." But we were given the radio frequency on which one could directly call Saßnitz. "

So I called the port at Saßnitz directly.

When asked if we could get in, the answer came: "You are asking me?"

Also I said: "Do I need to set a homeland flag?"

They replyed: "Which one?"

"Well, the one with the work tool on it". (It was black, red, gold with a hammer and a circle.)

New answer: "I do not see any such need."

OK. Then we come in unmarked.

The formalities were then gone through as in older times. The Coast Guard demanded to see all our passports and to have a full crew list. He then entered all data in his log form.

The Customs officer, on the other hand, was more open-minded. He drank a beer with us and told us the Coast Guard were to be dissolved, and so pretended there was much work for them to carry out, sheer pomposity!

The Customs officer also told me where we could go for a cheap meal and a hair cut, all in the fishing community of Saßnitz / Rügen. For ridiculously little money we enjoyed all the things it could offer, including the not bad Rostock beer.

The port itself offered a sad picture, only obsolete and rusted fishing vessels with ourselves in amongst them as the only white sailing yacht. After two days we left Saßnitz again to return to our home port of Laboe.

Charter Companies and Boat Dealers

We had to transfer a Feeling 1350 named "High Leverage" from Rodney-Bay on St. Lucia in the Caribbean to Palma de Mallorca. Myself, Lofoten Rudi, as skipper and two colleagues as the crew.

We were on a tight time schedule for the transatlantic crossing, so we had to hurry everywhere.

Furthermore we needed to load onto the ship, 10 sets of linen and 10 sets of diving equipment. The charter company in St. Lucia said it was all ready for us in the warehouse.

So, off to the warehouse.

The warehouse manager was a local coloured lady named "Pearl" who piled everything infront of us and said it was all ok.

From experience I was suspicious and started checking the piles. The first two stacks of linen were actually ok, but the rest, every stack was full of holes. The same for the diving equipment, flippers that did not match, goggles with no glass in them etc.

There was a hell of a kerfuffle, until everything was sorted and we could take it all away.

Everything was quickly stowed away and then off to Martinique, where we had ordered provisions from the ship chandler.

In Fort de France, the supplier was already on the pier and helped us to stow away the crates. It was then a case of paying the bills, taking on water and fuel, and setting off on the journey, first to an imaginary point 600 NM east of the Bermudas taking advantage of the strong Passat wind.

As we were unpacking the food containers, we realized that the supplier had deceived us. Cans were partly bulging, suggesting that the contents were tainted. Cardboard boxes with biscuits or hard bread had large holes where rats had chewed through in his warehouse. The contents had disappeared.

Useable amonst other things were a large sack of potatoes and a sack of onions. In addition, we had 15 fresh pineapples stored in the side racks to keep fresh air around them.

One morning I noticed that there were small bubbles appearing on the sides of the pineapples. They had started to ferment due to the hot climate. My fellow sailors thought they should be thrown overboard. I decided, however, that the bit of alcohol was not harmful and so there was always an obligatory thick disk for each of us in the mornings.

When the other useful provisions came to an end, there was nothing else until Gibraltar except: roast potatoes with onions in the morning, onions with fried potatoes at noon, fried potatoes with onions in the evening. The next day repeating the same thing again.

Despite these adverse circumstances, the crew enjoyed the trip and survived "undamaged".

A Night in the Cells

We had brought a Nauticat 52 from Lübeck over the Baltic Sea and through the canals to the boat exhibition in Dusseldorf.

After the show, the ship was to return to Wedel in Holstein.

The journey through all the canals with the many locks, some of which did not operate at the week-end, had been quite labourious.

In order to avoid this and the risk of ice which could be expected at this time of the year on the waters, I decided to go down the Rhine to get to the North Sea then up to the river Elbe.

We were only three on board, myself as a captain, my girl friend Sigi, and a colleague whom I knew from the Navy.

We sailed down the Rhine, fueled and bought food.

On the way it was dark with heavy snowfalls. We did not have radar, so we had to keep a concen-trated and sharp lookout in order not to get too close to the stone peirs built into the river.

We must have been around Emmerich on the Rhine, when suddenly a vehicle appeared next to us, which in addition to driving lights had blue flashing lights.

Then came the instruction:

Follow me!

So we followed the vehicle into the small port of Emmerich and pulled alongside.

It was a vehicle of the Dutch water protection police. They drew our attention to the fact that there was a sign on the shore with the inscription "Here, sport boats need to be to get clearance." The Schengen agreement was not yet in existence.

The next day I looked at the sign. It was small and dimly lit. So at night and with blowing snow not visible at all.

First of all, the passports please. They were all right, so we could have sailed on from the police.

In the stern of the boat, however, were now three gentlemen dressed in civilian clothes, and as it turned out, they were from the customs department.

They assumed immediately, despite my loud protestations to the contrary, that we wanted to import the ship illegally into Holland to sell it there.

Our colleague was allowed to stay on board to guard the boat. My girlfriend and I were arrested. Dressed as we were in oilskins and thick fur coats, we were brought ashore and detained in a cell while matters were clarified. In the cell it was stuffy and hot.

The next morning we were let out. In the office, the senior Customs officer was present. He issued us a fine of DM 3,000 which had to be paid (Euros had not yet been introduced).

I asked to make a phone call, because we did not possess the necessary T2 papers, which were at the customs in Germany.

So I called the owner in Germany and asked what to do.

He said the ship had already been sold so pay the penalty with a cheque, and get back as soon as possible.

I asked the chief officier if I could pay by cheque. He said that was possible.

So he watched me write the cheque for 3,000 DM in complete silence, then obviously hating our nationality, he tore the cheque up in front of my eyes and threw it in the waste paper basket.

Then he said, "Cash cheques can only be accepted up to a maximum of 300 DM per cheque."

My girlfriend and I filled out all our cheques. Together, we just had enough.

I asked: "May we now continue?"

He answered: "Yes, you can, but up river on the Rhine, back to Germany!"

As a farewell, they handed us a sugar-free coffee.

So began the canal odyssey again, with the same difficulties as the trip down until we finally arrived in Wedel.

Tricky Manoeuver

The shipyard of Portoferraio on Elba was a real challenge with the Mistral blowing up a storm.

The entrance was long and not very wide. One had to steer between two dams to get into the actual port.

With the Mistral, however, the strong wind blew across the entrance, which was not a problem with a good frontal approach.

The real problems began inside the actual port basin.

The port was small and full of ships. In order to berth „Roman Catholic" style, you had to stop the ship, line up in the correct position, then reverse back in a free berth equipped with mooring lines.

Without a bow thruster this was almost impossible. During a storm, the front of the ship was immediately pushed to the side before you could start to reverse back.

The ships did not yet have a bow thruster.

What to do?

So in the bay, before entering the harbor, take the anchor off the chain and release about 20 m of chain.

Then, with full reverse thrust, dragging the chain through the water and sediment, steer straight down the long entrance passageway directly into a free mooring.

Change to forward thrust to stop the ship. Then with stern lines deployed and mooring lines up front, the ship is fixed. Now reattach the anchor to the chain and the anchor in it´s holding. This maneuver is a "highlight" for onshore spectators despite the strong winds and often also the rain.

From the ship's captain, it requires courage, accurate knowledge of the maneuverability of his ship, as well as occasionally practicing in good weather.

Late Settlement

On a Gib-Sea Master 48, "Ventolera", on which I sailed as a captain and instructor, the following happened:

The ship had in the foredeck two double cabins, each with two berths, one above the other.

On one of these journeys the starboard cabin was occupied by a female lawyer in the upper bunk and an astronautical engineer in the lower one.

In an otherwise quiet night in a Mallorcan port, it happened that there was a huge dull blow in the foredeck, followed by an "animal" cry of pain.

What had happened?

Everyone was instantly awake!

As a responsible skipper, I quickly realized that the engineer had fallen out of the bunk and had a nasty cut on his leg which he must have caught on the catch of the door as he fell. The first need was to give medical help. Afterwards on serious reflection, I wondered, how was that possible? The lower bunk was at a lower level than the door catch. Strange, strange.

A three-quarters of a year later I received a card with a wedding announcement from both.

A Black Tag on the Card File

It was on a Sunday in the port of Portals on Mallorca.

As a DHH Captain on a Gib Sea M 48 called "VENTOLERA", I had my only day off, the new passengers were due to be embarked at 16:00h.

I lay down for a rest in my bunk and doze. At around 10:30h, a women's voice croaked from the Pier, she called out the ship Ventolera.

I was now up, stood in the corridor and gave her to understand that embarkation was only from 16:00h. But she persisted, she insisted on coming on board.

Not good.

She came aboard and said she had a present for me, a bottle of whiskey from the duty-free. I put it in the bottle rack to make it available to everyone on board.

At 16:00h everyone was embarked and I distributed cabins and bunks. Now it happens that this woman had share a cabin with a man in the front port, but in bunks. She objected to this vehemently.

For the sake of peace, the man agreed to sleep in the drawing-room. She now had a cabin to herself.

After eating ashore, we were still sitting comfortably in the mess with a glass of wine, during which Mrs. X slowly drank the whiskey she had brought earlier.

This, of course, had an effect, and when she fell out of her bunk during the night, she tore the hook off the door, tearing its fixings out of the wood. In the morning she appeared with the words: "Look what I have found here!"

After breakfast she went ashore to get some money from the bank.

We had planned to leave at 12:00h after briefing and security instructions. That had been made known to all but the woman was not back yet.

The engine was running, the crew stood clear on the lines and fenders, I allowed another half hour; then she came slowly down the pier and surprised us with the statement: "There was such beautiful coffee and cake on the way."

In the course of the trip, we ran into some bad weather on an inter-island crossing from Bonaire (Mallorca) to Ciudadela (Menorca).

Said "Lady" sat in the stern basket at the rear and was seasick. Suddenly she said she had to pee urgently.

I was at the helm and informed her of the various possibilities: "Below deck toilet, bottle in cockpit, etc." Because of sea sickness, she initially strictly rejected the toilet.

But as the pressure increased, she huddled under the deck to relieve herself with the door open to make it easier to remove her panties. Then she re-appeared on the deck.

We continued on the crossing when I sent some-one down to check our position. The crewman shouted back up the question: "Is it right that all floor boards are under water?"

Alarm!

I left the helm, and whirled below the deck.

"Activate the bilge pump immediately". The water was coming from the toilet. The "lady" had left open all the outboard valves. The danger was soon eliminated, but that was enough. I never wanted to see the woman again, so I asked the people in the booking office to mark her file with a black tag.

Impossible Seamanship

On a hot summer day we went into the port at Puerto Soller on Mallorca with our 48-foot "Ventolera" boat in the late afternoon.

The weather forecast of Palma-Radio had warned of severe thunderstorms.

In the summer, the ports of Mallorca are as full in the late afternoon as on the Baltic Sea.

At the concrete pier for excursion boats there were two berths still available for yachts moored aft end in to the pier „Roman Catholic" style. The water depth was 3,5 - 4 m.

So pulling up 50 m in front of the pier, I dropped anchor as we slowly backed up to the pier, keeping tension on the chain. Then over with the lines, check the anchor chain was stiff. Good anchorage, with 40 m laid out the chain could not extend a millimeter further. The anchorage was secure, we were safe for the night, even with the gusts in the u-shaped bay.

After half an hour another yacht of nearly the same size came into the harbor and saw the only remaining free berth next to us.

They tried first to go back and forth wildly and eventually came next to us with stern to the pier. The anchor was not deployed.

When I pointed out to the ship's skipper that use of the anchor was necessary and informed him of the weather report, I received several answers in Bavarian: "We are coming from "Starnberger See", we will do that later."

All right.

An hour later, an inflatable boat was lowered into water with one man in it. The 18 kg anchor was eased into the boat with some chain attached. The man in the boat was now trying to drag out the anchor with his rowing oars.

Anyone who has ever tried this knows that this is impossible. The weight of the chain pulls the boat back after every oar stroke. It does not work even with an outboard motor.

He threw the anchor about 5-6 m in front of the ship, he had given up. The chain now hung vertically from the bow, the inflatable was put back on the ship.

After a few evening drinks, we were all in the bunks, most were asleep, I was dozing awaiting the coming events. From time to time sheet lightning could be seen through the portholes.

It may have been about two o'clock, when the first violent squalls hit. Our ship tore at the chain and the additional securing lines.

My co-skipper Arno and I were immediately up on the deck in our underpants there was not time to don oilskins.

On the pier was total chaos and mortal danger. Everywhere tables and some iron garden chairs were flying through the air.

With a loud crash, the neighbouring boat rammed into the pier. Wood parts splintered, stainless steel bent, groaning, plastic outer skin was crushed. Her dinghy flew over our railing and landed firmly wedged between our mast and boom.

The crew of the adjacent ship had now appeared in pajamas on the deck and tried to stop the ship constantly crashing against the pier. Hopeless!

In the flash of the lightning you could see the walls of water crashing around the bay. Then the shouting of the neighbor's skipper: "What's happening?" Then he saw the dinghy which had landed on our ship, wedged into our rigging.

He shouted, "I have to moor onto your boat."

On a previous occasion in a Mistral storm in Macinaggio (Corsica) I snapped a ten gauge chain, but on a 42-foot ship. My answer was: "Only over my dead body!"

On this ship I currently had a twelve gauge-chain, but this ship was also 6 feet larger than the the one in Corsica. The responsibility for my ship and the crew lay with me.

One squall followed another, accompanied by lightning and thunder.

After an hour and a half as morning was beginning to dawn, the storm abated. We had not suffered any damage. Everything had held.

On the neighboring ship, the morning sun shone onto the foreshortened aft of the ship with its mess of bent stainless steel tubes which had once been railings and basket.

We handed over the inflatable boat, which had been torn during the night and was now deflated, to the boat alongside.

The lesson to be remembered from this extremely troubled night: "Seamanship also needs to be learned from the ground up."

The Chief Examiner

In the DHH sailing school on Elba, skipper proficiency tests were usually carried out every 14 days during the summer season. These were overseen in turn by the heads of the sailing schools located in the bay of Portoferrario. At that time the sailing license had three grades A, B. and C.

For us as a skippers and instructors it meant a 14-day training course, usually around Corsica, then two days of intensive training in the bay of Portoferrario followed by the test.

As an instructors, you knew all the examiners, their advantages and disadvantages, and in particular, their little quirks. One also tried to gently guide the more nervous students. All the inspectors in our area behaved pretty well the same at our respective berths in the shipyard. The address between the skippers and the inspectors was the informal "You".

The only exception to this was for the chief examiner, Herr ...., who often came across from Germany, a pure theorist. If one caught him, then the whole thing ran somewhat differently.

He came direct to the city port, had to be picked up at the Café Roma.

As a precaution we had already brought his favorite cigarette brand from Corsica, black filterless Gauloises, also because they were correspondingly cheaper there.

The ship lay then, in all weathers, according to "Roman Catholic" regulations, with an appropriate anchor at the pier.

He arrived on base, then followed his short speech, in a formal "You" form, which already brought some of the trainees into a sweat: "So you want to pass the test here. Good! The responsible ship's captain, however, is Mr. Neumann, he is responsible for the safety of his ship, so he must intervene if required for safety. If he should need to intervene, then you will have failed.

So let's start with Mr. / Mrs.........someone. Follow the commands given in accord with the regulations ..." etc.

Sometimes, when the Mistral was blowing heavily, he would choose to have the student turn into a small box bounded on both sides, which was hardly longer than his own ship, to see if the student was able to withstand the pressure without giving up. As said before, the ships in those days did not have bow thrusters.

If the captain of the ship complained that he would not be able to get out without help again, then a different maneuvering place was chosen.

After the maneuver, sail set, perform a few turns, respond to a man overboard situation, then the obligatory piece of paper came out of the trouser pocket, with a position within the bay and the instruction: "Sail there and set anchor at the exact position." This of course required the taking of many bearings, etc. In the case of C class tests, fresh instructions were issued after the anchor manoeuvre: "weigh anchor", then the new position reference came out of the other pocket, "sail to that position" outside the bay, and when you believe you are there, confirm it by taking a sun position reading. He wanted to see guidance and astro navigation.

With female students one noticed immediately, if it became "tense".

He then immediately switched his form of address from "Miss or Mrs whoever" to" Madam "and his stock phrases came out:

If the genoa sail had been flapping wildly rather than kept taut, he would say, "Madame needs to practice sailing close to the wind for a thousand miles. However if the desired goal is achieved, even by constantly tacking back and forth, over-working the crew, then I am obliged to give you a pass mark, for you have achieved your goal, but you will never win a race this way."

Behind his back, the skippers still had to bite their tongues every now and then whilst furtively correcting the steering, otherwise many manoeu-vers would have gone belly up.

After some years, some situations and people can often come back to the memory.

The Chief Examiner was unfortunately tragically lost in a car accident.

Arrested in Casablanca

During the transfer of two ships from the Mediterranean to the Canary Islands, we arrived in Casablanca just before midnight. A youth in a rowing boat took us to a berth on the side of a pontoon.

No sooner had we stopped and paid the boy when a gentleman in civilian clothes appeared on the pontoon. He showed his identity card and said he was a police inspector. He asked for the "captain"

I said it was me, then he said, "You are under arrest, follow me".

I went over to the ship and handed control over to another crew member.

I followed the Inspector and soon I did not know where we were.

We travelled through narrow streets, backyards and stables. He then called in at a bar where he met some "friends". He just let me wait.

After I had pointed out to him that I wanted to get back to the ship, he broke away from his cronies and we walked on.

At last we came into a bar on the first floor of a house. He ordered me to sit down at a table. Then he threw me a stack of forms, which he had fetched from a window-sill, and indicated to me: "Fill these in!"

Then he said, "Have something to drink!" I did not want anything, nor did I have any money with me due to the hurry.

I filled in the forms, which were written in French, as best I could.

Then he looked at them briefly, "Everything is wrong".

I told him that he could ask me the questions and I would give the correct answers. But he did not go down this route, instead he suggested that I should choose one of the "beauties" from around the counter. My thought was, "He is involved in all these *businesses*."

When I refused again and asked to return to my ship, he took the convoluted route back with me.

On the way he started again to work on me. Time after time he asked for whiskey, American cigarettes, US dollars, German marks, etc.

Finally we were back at the ship. I had refused to give him anything, but now I knocked on the deck. It was now four o'clock in the morning. My deputy appeared, and I asked him if he had a small sum of DM 10, somewhat concerned that the inspector would not be satisfied with it. But surprise, surprise, he pocketed the money reached into his back pocket, took out our Landing tickets, stamping them and handed them over to me. Then he disappeared.

What a performance for 10 DM.

Heavyweight

On a trip with a Gib. Sea. 442 "Tramontana" of the DHH school around the Balearic Islands, present on board, including me, were the following.

We were a group of seven, which included a construction engineer from a large construction company who was an absolute heavyweight. He may well have weighed in at around 140 Kg.

We were on the way around Mallorca about to pass the Cap Formentor and suddenly found ourselves in an emerging strong southwesterly with heavy gusts.

Quickly a short, very turbulent sea developed, which really shook the vessel lying on the wind, with every wave we hit. It was like hitting a concrete wall.

In the middle of this situation, the afore mentioned heavyweight felt a human need, he had to go to the toilet.

The toilet which was located on the starboard side in the foreship was designed for normal weight people and affixed to the side wall with an oblique flange. This construction proved to be too weak for the sudden load to which it was subjected as a result of both the swell and the immense body weight.

The bowl broke from its fixings and the contents of the "pan" spilled over the floorboards.

Fortunately the outboard valve was still closed; thus preventing a disaster.

The heavyweight escaped with a fright.

For me and the co-skipper this meant, after entering the port of Puerto Soller, a full day of laminating work and cleaning.

The rest of the crew meanwhile, were enjoying a trip in the country.

A Scare Tour

On a four-week DHH tour with the "Ventolera" from Mallorca via Sardinia, Ustica, Aeolian Islands, Stromboli, Strait of Messina, Taormina, Catania, Siracusa, Malta, Lampedusa, Pantelleria, Kelebia, Bizerte, Sardinia, Menorca and back to Mallorca the following occurred.

I had a crew change in Catania and was on the way to Lampedusa via Siracusa and Malta. A distance of well over 80 miles, which for a 48 foot ship with a good wind from the right direction is about a day sailing. With nine people on board, we had already passed through the Narrows between Malta and Gozo just as a thunderstorm with gales and heavy showers started up. Initially the sails were down and the engine was running. I tried to avoid the very strong winds and the water spouts. After surviving the thunderstorm, where luck was on our side, then despite the anxiety of the passengers, we set the sails, but fully reefed in, with the winds gusting seven to eight and variable in direction. So we continued on course to Lampedusa.

Shortly before the port the wind increased again. We just shot through the harbor entrance.

The port is small, on the onshore wind side berthing down was impossible. On the official police pier there was a lot of space with only two vehicles moored up, Guardia Finanza (Financial) and

Guardia Custodia (Customs). I tried to put it there. Immediately uniformed officials appeared and told us "get the hell out of here."

At the other end of the harbor was an extremely high quay wall, without a ladder. We moored up with the help of a kind soul on the quay in "Roman Catholic" position. It was a totally restless place. No one could disembark onto the landing quay.

After us came a large ferry boat, which laid up just behind the outer jetty on leeward side and fastened lines across the harbor entrance so we were trapped.

It was like riding on a roller coaster, bouncing up and down with constant grinding against the wall...

Dreadful!

No one could get off the ship, so the passengers were bored and started to moan.

The next day it was a bit more manageable. Around 10 o'clock the ferry loosed its mooring lines and left the port in the direction of Sicily.

Now the passengers began to complain. "It's boring, we can not go ashore, shit harbour, etc ..."

Ok, let's go, but turning was impossible, so we moved slowly from the mooring with lifevests on even in the port and a strongly reefed sail and so off we set.

Outside the harbour were monster waves coming from an odd angle as we headed for Pantelleria. We dropped down the high waves and made good progress. However, we were often submerged by the surging water.

The flat beach of the Island of Linosa quickly came up on the starboard side and disappeared immediately with the next squalls.

Some of the passengers were seasick and lay in the corners of the cockpit.

The wind turned to head-on, with a very rough cross-sea, which also slowed our progress.

Again and again thunderstorms came down with corresponding torrential rain, which meant we rode deep in the water.

My hope was to reach the port of Scauri on Pantelleria before nightfall. From experience and the port handbook I knew that the small harbor was problematic due to the surrounding cliffs and I did not want to try to dock at night.

The wind continued to turn, so we slowly sailed against the wind with some slack in the sail lines. The journey was a struggle against the sea all the time. Dusk was approaching along with more thunderstorms with torrential rain. Huge masses of water from above and below crashed upon us; in the far distance the outlines of the island and the first lights appeared.

Slowly we came closer, but it was now dark. Knowing the harbor, I hoped to spot the red light on the pier.

The passengers were terrified. With good seamanship it would have been possible to stay outside of the harbour till the light of day, but not with this unnerved crew.

Below deck, an older woman collapsed to the floorboards in a diabetic coma and had to be taken care of. It got worse. I had just glimpsed the faint red pier light when a lightning bolt hit the transformer station on the island, and all the lights, including the pier light were extinguished. Cascades of water still beat down at us, the sprayhood ripped. Meanwhile, we were now close to the island. Sails secured, engine running and radar on. I had asked a flight instructor to closely monitor the radar, and to let me know if he could make out the pier to give me the bearing.

To my repeated question: "Do you see anything?" always the same answer: "I see nothing."

But somehow I needed to at least catch sight of the red pillar on which the red light was installed. So to the hand spotlight on the deck. In the beam of the lamp, nothing could be detected at first in the downpour. Sweeping back and forth over the horizon. Stop, there was something to be seen despite the rain. Thanks to my knowledge, I managed to reach the small safe harbor.

My radar operator had not been able to find anything because the device had been set to cover too large an area.

After clearing up the ship, I needed a stiff drink, the passengers just disappeared to their bunks.

Looking back at all that had happened, this had been a terrible trip.

The Examiner from Bodensee (Lake Constance)

The sailing school in Laboe, wanted me to undertake a training trip around Skagen.

We were using a Moody yacht with the owner on board. He intended to sail this home himself after completing the test for his C-class license.

The other participants were BK and BR aspirants. Before leaving, the owner said he was already a trained seaman, so he did not need anything but instruction and testing in astro navigation.

After we had clarified who was to act as ship's skipper and who was in charge and got the final say, he asked if he could continue to occupy his owner's cabin at the rear of the ship.

I did not mind because I preferred the bunk with the chart table.

So we set off, through the great belt, then up the Kattegat to finally get into the Skagerrak. The hard swell put the ship to the test. Some were seasick, including the owner, who remained in his chamber. Together with the rest of the crew, I continued the training in theory and practice despite the weather conditions. After rounding Skagen, the owner appeared once again still looking ashen.

Since he did not need anything else, we focussed on plotting and sailing a few different courses. This was achieved by using the sextant to measure the angle of the sun, recording the readings and thereby calculating our position.

From Jammerbugt, a wide bay on the west coast of Jutland, the wind continued to increase reaching force 8 winds but blowing from a favorable quarter. At high speed we "thundered" in the direction from Jutland to Heligoland.

Taking turns at the helm, the crew were now ready for the sea. The high-speed ride with wind behind pushed us rapidly forward, the mood was quite positive with maybe just a little anxiety.

Sometimes the owner came out of his chamber, only to disappear immediately. I did not care, he had his courses to plot, he did not need to know more.

We reached Heligoland very quickly, took a break for a day to recover and then set off to return via the river Elbe and the Kiel Canal.

On the Baltic Sea, we moved to Damp 2000, where the test was to take place.

The day of the test came. The examiner was the well known Captain Y....

"We first test BK and BR," the examiner said, "and then the C- man."

So we went out and followed the usual maneuvers: tack, jibe, tighten, man overboard, and always a few questions about the seamanship and knots. Ultimately, all had passed.

Now came the C-man's turn.

He immediately expressed the opinion that as he had already passed his seamanship competency exams he only needed to be tested in Astronavigation.

But he had not reckoned on Captain Y...., who had himself sailed with big sailing ships. The practical maneuvers did not go very well, far from perfect, and we finally headed back in to port.

Then fate took its course

Captain Y.... did not want to check the base records following on from the skipper, Mr. N.... nor did he want to see them. He said, "If N.... says the candidate has passed his skippers exam that is o.k., but I still have a few general questions:

When you have the C-License then you are able to sail on all the world's oceans.

Now, imagine, you are coming across the Atlantic and wanting to enter the mouth of the river Elbe (he specified a date and time). As you are a little off position, you are near the corner of the great sandbank. Now tell me, when can you pass and when not? "

There was no answer.

He said nothing to suggest he knew that there were certain books. He had no idea of tidal tables and had never heard of an atlas of tidal currents.

So it went on.

Finally Captain Y.... already hot under the collar, lost his temper and exploded, "You dare to present yourself here, you have no idea, and you are too stupid!"

Thus the C-license examination was failed.

Conclusion: Examiners from Lake Constance do not know everything and should not be too full of themselves.

Midst of War

In the year 2000 I was on a round tour of Mallorca lasting twelve weeks, with the "Ventolera", a 48-foot sailing yacht through the Mediterranean and the Black Sea, we had arrived in Constanta (Romania), with a group of nine people on board. Previously in Catania and Istanbul we had taken a fresh group on board and were now on the way to the Crimea peninsula. In the Crimea, we first headed for Balaklava where, at set time, we were to meet up with a Russian twin mast yacht at a pre-arranged position five miles outside the port entrance.

After reaching the position, there was now a dense fog, no one was there. Also on the radar there was nothing to discern. Calls on channel 16 produced no response.

After a while, my cell phone suddenly rang and a female voice said in very Old German:

"Mr. Rudolf (my first name), the Russian yacht is not coming, it is in the shipyard in Nicolajevsk, do not enter Balaklava, the naval harbor is blocked. Sail to Sevastopol and wait there for a white motorboat for clearance. Before that however, report to the coastal radio station Lebet Seven. "

"OK. All right, let's go the twelve miles to Sebas-topol. "

But first on channel 16:

"LEBET SEVEN, LEBET SEVEN, this is German sailing yacht Ventolera, how do you read, over"

No Answer.

The call was repeated.

This time an answer in strange English.

"Which flag do you fly?"

I replied:

"German flag and we are bound for Sebastopol."

Answer:

"OK. Go ahead, out. "

Two miles from the harbor we meet with a ship, the size of a frigate and armed accordingly, but with a white hull and the inscription "Ukrainian Coastguard". It sailed around us once, but did not speak to us, then disappeared towards the black sea.

Arriving at the port there is a strong swell so I sail through the outer break waters and move out of the main shipping channel in the outer harbour outside the line of green buoy`s to wait for the white motorboat.

Suddenly, two minesweepers with equipment deployed emerge out of the inner harbor, followed by a large landing craft

Having drawn level with us, from one of the minesweepers, an officer shouted something in Russian from the bridge yardarm which we did not understand. After that a loud bang. One fired * "Chaff" (= Large clouds of tinfoil that are intended to distract missiles) into the air and the empty large shellcases hit the water five or six meters from our ship. The Landing craft opened its hatch, many floating tanks emerged firing from all barrels. On the pier, T 72 tanks were lined up set to fire to sea. At low level, Mig's whizzed over us, it was like being in the middle of a war.

A rowing boat appeared with a boy in it, but he kept his distance and the boy shouted, "Captain, Captain you are running into danger, follow me."

Slowly we followed the boy into the calmer waters. The war continued in the harbour. Cruisers fired rockets at sea, frigates followed on, at the rear sat an atomic submarine. All the time circled by bombers, hunters and combat helicopters. It was a huge spectacle.

After one and a half hours, the nightmare was over and we dared to approach the shipping channel again.

Then the motorboat we had been awaiting appeared with seven men and an interpreter on board. We had to follow into a specially shielded dock, moor up and then they all came on board to us.

The head of the uniformed troop began the interrogation:

"Captain, how did you get to enter into a locked naval harbor?"

I explained it to him and submitted my logbook. He took careful notes. The poor man on the coast station!

After that came the veterinarian's turn.

"Captain, where is your rat certificate?"

"We are a sailing yacht, we have no rats on board and therefore no certificate!"

"Captain, every ship has rats aboard, if you say nothing then you need another form."

Well then.

First question in the new form. "What health consequences did you notice during the journey due to the rats?"

This is nonsense and probably does not need to be answered.

Polite but determined: "Captain, please you have to fill in"!

So it went on for over three hours non-stop.

How many guns, how much gunpowder, how much gold, I thought of ingots, not jewelery and wedding rings. How much money? I guessed in total about 2000 dollars.

No of course not! I had traveled through many countries and had a variety of currencies, and the crew also had different money in their pockets. So make a pile, count it all, enter it onto the list and yet again the reminder:

„Captain, please you have to fill in"!

Then everything was sealed with a ship's stamp. We acknowledged that we understood everything regarding the content. Furthermore, we waited for an additional 24 hours listening to channel 16 to ensure all was safe, etc., then the nightmare was over.

We choose to take a break form listening, and at the gate post we found there was always an open gap and so we went through and had a wonderful time in the best restaurant with great food and drinks at very reasonable prices and excellent views over the entire naval harbor.

It was followed by excursions and museum visits, before we sailed on to Yalta after three days.

A Strange Owl

In the 1990s, I spent several winters, when there was no sailing in Europe, in Costa Rica and Panama.

Among other things, I skippered for guests on a heavily built wooden ketch of 16 m called "EL VIEJO" (the old) on behalf of the company Bavarian Motors (BMW) Panama.

After each arrival of the guests at the TUCUMAN-Airport, we travelled by Land Rover to Panamá City to their hotel. Next day, visit to Panama Viejo, Colonial Panamá and the Mira Flora lock on the canal, after which we would set off for Colon, 80km away, where the ship was berthed at the Panama Canal Yacht Club.

After replenishing the boat we sailed from the Limon Bay to Porto Belo, and then via Isla Grande upstream to the San Blas Islands. Columbus had already said: "more islands than days in a year".

In the nineties, these islands were not so well known, as the magazines had not yet taken up the issue. We spent 14 wonderful days here.

On one of these trips we came again to "PANETUP", an island, that is rather a bay, which is surrounded by several small islands and thus very protected.

Apart from us, there was only one very strange ship in the bay. I manned the big rubber dinghy we were towing and motored over to the ship. It was not really a ship in our sense. It was no more than 6 m long and had a round barrel-like super-structure with a "cheese bell" on top.

As we approached, the lid of this box opened and a little man of, I guess, 80 years of age peeked out and beckoned to me to come alongside.

I did that and he greeted me with "join me for a cup of tea."

When the tea was ready, I continued to sit on my dinghy, because the oversized "bread tray" had room for only one. He told me that he had travelled with this vessel for years to all corners of the world. He was an Englishman and said he had become a little tired of traveling. At the end of the "tea party" we said goodbye. His last sentence was: "I will cross the Atlantic now for the last time and drop my anchor in the cabbage garden."

OK. Have a nice trip. I motored back to "El Viejo".

Note: The Cabbage Garden was an old burial ground in Dublin, Ireland

Under Pirates

It was the time when the "drug baron" Noriega was still ruling in Panamá, everything was a bit haywire.

The drug trail from Colombia via Central America to the US seemed to work. In Panama life was somewhat dangerous at this time. A particularly bad patch was, for example, the port city of Colon, at the entrance of the Panama Canal on the Caribbean side.

I was once again hired to sail with guests on the "El Viejo" in the San Blas Islands.

Even the shopping in the supermarket in Colon was always adventurous.

Security guards everywhere with shotguns or submachine guns.

When bulk buying supplies, we usually had 5-6 trolleys full, and often carried 500 - 600 $ US in cash, which was a rarity in Colon.

The lady at the cash register rang the bell immediately for the manager and three heavily armed men moved in.

As a rule, we paid in $100 banknotes, which were first checked for authenticity by the manager through a scratch-check procedure.

After that, all goods were quickly loaded into our car and we set off at high speed for the Panama Canal Yacht Club, where our ship El Viejo was berthed.

For protection against raids, I was given a shotgun and a pistol with 16-rounds of ammunition by the company which hired me to sail their guest visitors. I always stashed both under my mattress.

The journey started as normal. The Passat wind was very strong and we made good progress on our usual route.

So Porto Belo, Isla Grande, Porvenir, La Lunega, Chichime, Hollandeses, Panetup, Diatup and again Porvenir, then return to Colon via Isla Grande and Porto Belo.

So we were anchored at Porvenir when shortly after noon a somewhat run-down Columbian schooner appeared and moored at the small island pier.

They off-loaded coconuts, whether for real or for purposes of deception. The strong crew looked very ragged. At four o'clock in the afternoon they began to drink and roared loudly.

My guests were worried and I had to calm them.

It was getting dark and my guests disappeared to their bunks. I too was a little worried. The rowdiness continued on the Columbian ship.

Suddenly, it must have been around midnight - I was now flat out on the cockpit bench and had the shotgun and pistol ready to hand next to me – The schooner moved and anchored about 20-25 m away next to us. On her foredeck lay a canoe which was ready for immediate use.

What to do if they came now?

I considered my options, I did not want to open fire directly at them, but, if they actually appeared, then I would at first shoot over their heads as a deterrent.

They continued to drink and could be heard laughing. Then it all became quiet, they must have fallen asleep. When the morning dawned, they raised the anchor, set their sails and disappeared.

Before my guests were awake I had stowed the weapons again, the nightmare was over. My night's sleep also.

SAME SHIT EVERY DAY (or Rescue from the Caribbean)

On board "EL VIEJO", a wooden heavy ketch, we lay at anchor in the San Blas archipelago, Panamá, behind an outer reef of the island Panetup.

During the night, the northeast trade wind had increased vigorously with wind forces running to 7-8, such that a high sea had formed outside the reef in the open sea.

In the morning hours, the wind slowed down a bit and we raised anchor to sail to the Cayos Hollandes.

When we emerged from the shelter of the island, we sailed out onto the rough sea. We nevertheless made good progress with reefed sails.

The boatman Bernal re-emerged from the stairwell having been briefly below deck, he looked all round.

Suddenly he shouted: "There was something there"!

There were only the two of us on board and I stood at the long tiller and steered the ship. At first I could not see anything out of the ordinary. Then he screamed again, "There," pointing in a certain direction.

Now I saw it too. Some distance away, an arm temporarily popped out of the water on a crest, swinging a rag.

We immediately changed our course and edged closer to the spot.

Now we could see that there were four KUNA Indians floating in the water and next to them only the nose of a canoe sticking out of the water.

There were three teenagers and one old Indian. Since there were only the two of us on board, the rescue operation was extremely difficult.

The ship was lumbering in this swell, with our large rudder and long heavy two man tiller trying to get through the wind. All maneuvers had to be performed during a jibe.

At the second attempt, one of the younger men succeeded in reaching up the "El Viejo" to seize our rigging shrouds and get on board.

Now with three of us, we managed to get the old man aboard on the next maneuver. Completely exhausted, he simply remained lying at the stern.

In another attempt we got the last two boys out of the water.

They asked us to recover the canoe because it had a borrowed outboard engine.

Back round again. One of the boys jumped into the water and tied a towline to the canoe. As it turned, a piece of wood splintered from the gunwale, but then it followed in our wake.

Now the Indians told us that they were fishing two days ago and were caught in the storm. The canoe was badly battered, their catch and their fishing gear were lost.

For two days and nights they had drifted in the stormy sea. The water was warm, but the old man was completely exhausted. We gave them drinks, food and took them to the Hollandes Islands.

Arriving on the islands, they emptied out their canoe and with the help of our tools they got their outboard motor operational again.

Before they left us, they thanked us heartily for the rescue and support.

The old man had also regained his strength. They put him in their canoe, the sun had dried his totally faded and tattered T-shirt. While they were reasonably happy about it, one could see the faint lettering on his chest:

"SAME SHIT EVERY DAY"

The Error

On my sailing trips it sometimes happened that I unexpectedly encountered stray floating debris, some of which had to be collected when resulting from an emergency or distress situation. These were usually round tubing or plastic boats with and without outboard motors.

Among them were also new and used pedal boats with or without people on board. Where they were manned it was by reckless people who had strayed too far away from the coast in strong off-shore winds, now making no progress against the wind and waves. At times I would find them 5-10 miles off the coast in great distress and needing to be towed back to shore.

On one occasion, the story was completely differ-ent. Sailing on the "VENTOLERA" a 48 foot yacht with a crew of nine, we were headed from Mallorca on the way to Alicante on the mainland.

The weather was good, the wind blowing force 3-4 from SE, but with a pretty high swell.

Slowly we came upon another sailing yacht, which behaved in a particularly strange manner.

Through the telescope one could see that both the main and foresail were deployed, so a down wind course was being followed.

The ship was constantly yawing so that the sails frequently slapped back.

Obviously nobody was at the helm, nobody could be seen anywhere.

Could the ship be sailing here without a master? What would that mean for us? Thoughts circled in the crew. An abandoned ship? We would have to take care of it. We hoped, no illness or death.

We would have to either take it in tow or put together a skeleton crew, but first of all to determine who might have been on board.

Check for missing persons reports etc.

As the distance dwindled, you could see the French flag, but nobody was on deck.

Had the helmsman fallen overboard? So it was time to get closer.

The situation did not change, everything seemed quite strange.

Maybe help was needed, or in case of salvage, perhaps you could get a reward from the insurance?

In any case, first prepare for the maneuver.

That meant taking down the sails, starting the engine, putting out the fenders and laying out the towing equipment. An athletic crew member was assigned as a jumper.

Finally we were just 10 m away. Repeated calls produced no answer, surely nobody on board.

So we went alongside, and our man jumped over with a great, skilful movement.

The impact on the deck obviously disturbed someone in a precarious situation, because suddenly a man's head appeared in the companionway of the ship and shouted to us "Bonjour", while at the same time we saw through the porthole window of the deck a distraught naked woman scurrying by.

"Excusé monsieur, qu'est-ce que cést? Je pense, le Capitan est mort-vous émouvez pas, nous voulons les premiers aide, faire la courte échelle. "(Excuse me Monsieur, what is the matter? I think that the Captain is dead – you don't respond. We offer first aid, make the short crossing.)

The perplexed gentleman replied: "No, no merci Monsieur. Bon Voyage ".

Quickly we brought our man back on board and continued our journey.

A "Phenomenon" Appeared

In the autumn of 1993, I once again made one of the sailing trips I had often made before around the Balearic Islands. I was to skipper a proven ship, a Gib Sea 442 named "Tramontana".

The weather offered the normal autumnal conditions, that is winds from different quadrants, in strengths varying from 1-7, sun, clouds and sometimes a strong thunderstorm with corresponding gale gusts, so a normal autumn trip.

The route was as is often the case counterclockwise around all the islands of the Balearic Islands. We would visit many ports and anchor in various bays. Our starting port was the marina at Puerto Portals, near Palma. The crew consisted of two women, five men, plus myself as skipper, so a full ship.

So what was different then this time? Well shortly after leaving the port of Portals, it turned out that we had three Hornblower fans on board, namely Reiner, Artur and myself.

It is the novel series by Cecil F. Forester with the titles: 'Mr Midshipman Hornblower', 'Lieutenant Hornblower', 'Captain Hornblower', 'Hornblower in the West Indies' and ends with the book 'The King's Admiral'.

The contents of these books are modeled on the biography of the famous British naval hero Lord Nelson.

Since the English had occupied the Balearic island of Menorca for 80 years for the second largest natural harbor in the world at that time and the castle on Cabrera had served as a backdrop for a Hornblower film, we three connoisseurs reveled in our knowledge of the subject matter.

Some passages of the individual volumes were recited, each seeking to outdo the other

Often it was also debated, what would Mr. Bush (first Offz. Hornblower) have said, in all probability, regarding this maneuver as performed by us. The dinghy was suddenly transformed into Commander Gig. Compass grades have been converted to stroke division and much more. Even at dinner one believed oneself to be in the cabin on the "Lydia" or another of the ships. Even the food was called accordingly. So pudding a la "Lady Barbara" etc.

Passing the ancient fortifications of Mahon, Lazaretto Quarantine Station, Bloody Island, where hundreds of British sailors had limbs cruelly amputated after battles, all of this located in the natural harbour of Mahon, the enthusiasm of the "Hornblowers" flying particularly high. The former governor's palace on starboard was a further source of speculation. The governor was back then Lord Hamilton. How was it possible for the Sea Lord to approach the lady?

So it went on cheerfully, the brains turning over constantly, it culminated in that when we lay in a quiet bay at anchor and the cabin mate of Artur returned to his bunk after going for a pee, Artur exclaimed in dreamlike state, half asleep in the dark: "Hornblower, is that you "?

A Year „illegal" in Tunisia

On a journey from Mallorca via Menorca, Sardinia, Sicily, Malta, Pantelleria, Tunisia, we sailed from Scauri (Pantelleria) with the Gib Sea M 48 "Ventolera" and arrived in the afternoon in Kelibia (Tunisia).

As the skipper, I collected the passports, and the ship's papers and with my deputy went to the harbor office to report.

We were in a hurry because some of the crew wanted to come ashore quickly to exchange money before the banks closed. Without a landing ticket there would have been difficulties.

The port office had a uniformed policeman who checked our passports and ship's papers and filled out a form for each member of the crew. Afterwards he stamped the passes and the tickets and handed them to us. Everyone's that is except for my passport. He made me understand that I was under arrest. Why this was he did not say. My Arabic was not enough either.

First, I gave the passports and tickets to the deputy so that the crew could go ashore.

The policeman was busy talking on the phone and after half an hour a bicycle stopped in front of the door and a uniformed police officer entered the office. Both talked intensely in Arabic and the 2nd officer also told me that I was under arrest.

Now the officer picked up the phone and talked to someone for a long time. In between, I always tried to figure out why I was arrested, but got no answer.

It took about another hour, then the brakes of a car squealed outside and a man in civilian clothes entered the office. Under his baggy jacket, I easily realized that he wore a large-caliber weapon in his armpit holster. He had to be of a higher rank, as both uniformed men immediately stood to attention, maybe something like secret state police. After another long conversation, the civilian told me to sit down, gave me paper and pens, and said in French, as far as I could understood, that I should write a report explaining where I had spent a year illegally in Tunisia.

Since I had not stayed in Tunisia, I refused, but still speaking in English, „in which language please?" His answer: "In Arabic, alternatively in French". Both languages are not my strengths.

At first I did not understand how they came to believe that I had been illegally in Tunisia for a year and strongly demanded that I speak with the German Embassy.

But suddenly it dawned on me that I had been in Bizerte (Tunisia) a year ago by ship, maybe it was related to that.

I tried to make that clear to the civilian, because something did not seem to be correct with the departure in the passport. I could not read the Arabic script in the stamps. In broken English, he tried to make it clear to me that Tunisian officials were very conscientious and never made mistakes. However, he then gave the order to the hierarchy in Bizerte to check that a year ago a ship named "Ventolera" had both checked in and out.

It took another eternity before the phone rang again and the positive response came. Someone had obviously forgotten to put the exit stamp in my passport.

Then the civilian himself seized the phone and there was a cannonade of curses and insults in Arabic, which fortunately I did not understand.

After that, the order came down through the hierarchical ladder to turn the stamp back one year to confirm the departure, then restore it to the current date to document the re-entry.

My passport was up to date and I was released from custody after three and a half hours.

We were able to continue the journey and return via Bizerte, Cagliari (Sardinia), Mahon (Menorca) to our homeport Portals in Mallorca.

Buccaneer's Successor

On a voyage in 2001 with the sailing yacht "Ventolera" on which I sailed as a skipper, the following happened.

We sailed from Mallorca in several stages via first Gibraltar, then on to Cadiz, Mazagon, Ayermonte, Faro and then a crew change in Vilamoura.

From Vilamoura via Lagos and Sines to Lisbon.

Then carried by a strong Portuguese Northerly in a very fast drive first to Porto Santo and then to Funchal on Madeira. On the way back to the Mediterranean, we went directly to Casablanca, and then continued north along the African west coast towards Tangier.

On this course between Rabat and Tangier we came into a region of complete calm with no wind, thanks to a region of high-pressure.

It was late afternoon, the beating sails were lowered, the engine started and the journey continued.

The daylight was fading, it was getting dark, the water was like liquid lead, only the normal Atlantic swell was felt. We operated the usual watch system, that is there were two people on each watch. At 20:00 Hrs there was a change of watch personnel. The visibility was good, lights of vehicles far away could be seen, and also there was the additional light from the half moon.

Everything followed a normal routine, the engine purred, the watch were instructed as to course etc. It had to be manually controlled because we had no self-steering system. So I went to my room and dozed by myself. Quietly I heard the conversation of the watch crew in the cockpit. Sometime around midnight the conversations stopped, that was suspicious, I had to check things out.

I raced into the companionway, looked around and saw in the moonlight, the string of buoys supporting a steel mesh tuna fishing net, just ahead of the bow. I literally dropped onto the engine throttle and put it in reverse "full". But it was already too late, we ploughed into the steel net, the propeller caught the wires, the engine stopped immediately.

The monotony and lack of concentration had obviously caused the watch guard to fall asleep. Bawling them out was not going to help at this time.

The ship hung with keel and rudder trapped in the net. The shaft could not be engaged. In the Atlantic swell, the steel mesh was constantly tearing at the shaft and rudder. We were cruelly trapped and could not do anything.

The crew, now completely on deck, were paralyzed.

At the far end of the net, the lights of a net guard were visible far out. Slowly he left his position and came towards us. It was a terrible steel barge with a powerful engine.

When approached, they came out with a repertoire of curses in Arabic. Then they switched to Spanish and shouted: "Necesitamos una cuerda!" (We need a rope!).

In the dark, I reached into a stern box and pulled out the new, first-class 35-meter reserve line for hoisting the spinnaker and hurried forward. I threw the line to them and before I could secure it and get out of the way, they tore on the line to pull us out of the net.

The line dragged over the back of my hand and my forearm resulting in rope burns. Also my watch disappeared outboard. After that I had the line secured. Brutally they tore us from the net.

We were free again! Now came the second act. They shouted: "Quita la cuerda", so unfasten the line. Actually they should have unfastened and cast off, after all, it was our line. So I said, "No."

They cursed again, gave their engine some gas and rammed us at an acute angle to starboard, so that our footrail was pushed inwards. On my renewed: "No" there was a second more violent ramming which also damaged the anchor reeling. I believe that they would have continued till we sank. With a heavy heart, I decided to sacrifice the good line and set off. Then they disappeared with the prey.

We could now continue our journey. Repairs were carried out with on-board resources. The guilty crew who had been on watch that night bought me a new wristwatch in Gibraltar.

After reaching the home port we would later discover that the damage to the underwater area of the ship was limited. Apart from color abrasions nothing else had happened.

It was the fault of the crew, which had led to the accident, the assistance provided, or recovery, however, resembled an act of modern piracy.

The Treasure Hunters

In 1988, I received a phone call and a voice asked me in broken German if I knew anything about Costa Rica and could I get a ship there and skipper it.

When I answered positively, he introduced himself as a lawyer from Costa Rica and said that it was about a photo safari and gave me a Hamburg (Germany) phone number that I should call.

I made contact and we arranged an appointment.

At the meeting in a district of Hamburg, I met two German engineers who allegedly wanted to do a photo safari to the Cocos Island in the Pacific.

Since I was familiar with the sea area including the islands belonging to Costa Rica and could get a ship, we agreed on a contract and fixed the departure date.

Meanwhile, I spoke with my friend, who owned the ship called "El Viejo", and arranged for the man at the boatyard, to buy provisions and to make the ship seaworthy.

So we flew from Hamburg to San Jose, the capital of Costa Rica.

When leaving Hamburg I noticed some strange things among their luggage, a rifle bag, a case with heavy elongated content and so on, unusual at least for a photo safari.

We stayed overnight in San Jose and drove to Punta Arenas the next day, where "El Viejo" was in the marina on the Pacific coast.

Here also one of the local lawyers appeared on board.

The Isla de Coco is one of the national parks of Costa Rica and may be visited and entered only with official permission, so the lawyer was to be an official supervisor on board.

The ship was ready to sail, we set off and sailed down the Gulf of Nicoya, passing Cabo Blanco and went on the 350 nautical miles journey to the Isla de Coco.

The weather conditions were not the best, sometimes little wind, lots of rain and strong currents. In this region run the North equatorial current and the equatorial countercurrent.

Many ships have therefore missed the island in overcast skies. GPS did not yet exist!

However, I still managed to get a few sun position measurements and so on the afternoon of the 4th day the island came into sight and we entered into the Wafer Bay. There was a considerable swell at anchor.

When everyone was in the cockpit at night, I had already checked the strange pieces of luggage. Instead of rifles and photo tripods, there were crowbars, chisels and mallets, this was not equipment that went well with a photo safari.

Both engineers were sleeping in the foredeck, and at night you could hear them muttering at times.

In the morning after breakfast, both of them asked to use our dinghy to start their safari.

Since there was quite a heavy swell in the bay, I declined because neither of them were experienced seamen.

Strangely enough, they refused categorically for me or the boatman to go with them to handle the dinghy.

So I suggested we take the El Viejo around the island as the boatman wanted to go fishing, and then to drop anchor in Chatham Bay.

They agreed, we raised the anchor and sailed around the island.

Suddenly, at a spot where two uniform ridges could be seen sticking out of the water, known as the "Dos Amigos", they stared frantically at a certain spot on the island and whispered to themselves:

"That's it, we found it!"

After rounding the island, we anchored at Chatham Bay.

During the trip, the boatman had caught a nice wahoo (a large torpedo-like food fish), which was now prepared.

The night fell and in the forecastle once more the whispers began.

When the next morning dawned, they again energetically demanded to use the dinghy.

The weather and the strong swell had remained the same, so that I again vehemently refused.

Now they finally came out with the truth, they did not want to do a photo safari, but were looking for the Lima church treasure and believed to have found the place where it was hidden.

To make sure that I did not cheat them and recover the treasure for myself, they offered me a contract.

During the night they had drafted a document, it said that after deduction of all costs I should receive 10% of the proceeds.

The lost treasure to date is said to consist of thirty tons of gold, silver and precious stones, so a pretty penny.

I read the historical story after I returned.

So they believed that they had found the place of the hidden treasure which emerged from a mysterious puzzle and whose bearings they now gave to me.

Unfortunately, the information did not make sense and was not consistent with traditional navigation bearings.

As a navigator I set to work and recalculated the errors in the bearings back in time and lo and behold, now the bearings made sense.

Thereupon, the two men were almost impossible to hold back.

Our dinghy was small and not entirely safe in the swell.

So I decided to take the risk with the younger of the two and go to the calculated location.

On the way we were attacked by frigate birds and boobies who had their nests in the rock niches. It was like being in the movie by Hitchcock "The Birds".

I steered and the second man fought off the swooping birds with a plastic bowl.

We reached the alleged location in a cauldron surrounded by rock walls. The water foamed from the incoming surf and you could see the fins and outlines of tiger sharks.

In a corner of the rocks, I could make out the contours of a linden leaf-shaped stone, as it was described in the puzzle, presumably with a hole on one side, in which, according to tradition, a pole could be inserted to twist the stone. So one could then get into an old Inca cave, in which the treasure was hidden.

I had my doubts, because the outline could have originated naturally and the supposed hole could also be a tuft of grass.

Below the spot was a small rock platform, but it was washed over by the constantly thundering waves.

A landing was ruled out as impossible. We would have been smashed against the rocks.

The alternative of jumping into the water and trying to get onto the platform when it was just free of the water, was not something my fellow passenger dared to attempt, because of the danger and the sharks orbiting us.

He took only a few Polaroid photos and we motored back.

The weather did not improve, our time was limited, so we started the return journey to Puntarenas and finally back to Germany.

In Germany, the two contacted Christie's auction house, claiming to have found the treasure, and showed the pictures.

However, solid evidence was missing and the representative of Christies said: "Bring us a piece of the treasure, then the salvage is no problem.

That's why we sat on the plane fourteen days later and the tour started again.

We arrived at the island. I went with the older of the two to the supposed place. This time he had better camera equipment and he shot several photos.

However, the weather conditions were the same as on the first trip. Mighty surf shot into the small bay and thundered up the rock walls. A landing was again ruled out.

We returned to Germany without any useful results.

After that, I suggested that they get professionals in Germany, who could make a landing with appropriate equipment.

Both categorically refused to share the information with any more people.

For me, another trip was out of the question, as I had great doubts about the site.

In the further course of things, they nevertheless tried again. In addition I arranged for them to hire a fishing vessel with a strong dinghy.

As it turned out later, the weather conditions were more favorable and a third man managed to land at the site.

The supposedly linden leaf-shaped stone he worked at for a long time and the hole in the corner actually did turn out to be a tuft of grass.

From the dream of the big treasure!

I still have the contract to this day as a reminder and I live well, even without the appropriate share.

The sailing, however, was very interesting, but the great treasures that are still hidden on earth, do not fall into our lap so easily.

Dangerous Encounters

In 1977, during a Whitsun regatta from Heligoland to Granton Harbor / Edinburgh, we came with "Kallisto", a Swan 36, sailing in dense fog near to the island named "Isle of May" at the entrance to the Firth of Forth.

Using radio direction finding (GPS, DECCA, LORAN, etc. did not exist yet), we had the island directly ahead with their lighthouse and radio beacon.

As a navigator, I was constantly checking the ID and echo from the beacon.

The echo was very wide, so we were still a fair distance from island lighthouse and radio beacon. No foghorn was heard yet.

Suddenly the guard in the cockpit shouted, "There's the lighthouse!"

Impossible with the broad echo from the radio beacon.

I rushed up and immediately recognized through the fog the signal SHORT SHORT LONG given with a spotlight, so not the lighthouse identifier flashes, but the letter "U"

From the Morse code meaning "You are running into danger".

As a naval officer I immediately assessed the situation as we came closer.

It was a naval vehicle and an English minesweeper of the "Ton class" with discharged KFRG (cable remote sweeping device). This is a machine for clearing magnetic mines. The minesweeper pulls a large spool, which is in a hollow tube (looks like a small submarine), on a 500 to 1000 meters long cable behind her. In the coil, a strong magnetic field is set up with 30,000 volts to explode magnetic mines.

We were heading directly toward this cable and so in extreme danger!

Since we were on a course high on the wind, we were able to promptly turn and pass the fast moving minesweeper close on the bow and so at the last minute avioded the serious danger.

We were able to continue our journey without further difficulty.

Years later, in 1989, I was a skipper on the "Libeccio", a Gibs Sea 442. We were on a training trip from Elba to complete a circuit around Corsica.

Around lunchtime we ran into clear sunny weather "Kaiserwetter" about two nautical miles distance from the Corsican east coast. We had bright blue sky, sunshine and a light wind from the east of strength 2.

I went below deck to fill in the log book at the chart table.

I had turned down the volume on the VHF radio tuned to channel 16, it had become annoying with only a few ladies exchanging recipes.

When going below deck I had spotted a ship, which was clearly far away and stationary, so we would pass it at a safe distance.

During my work, however, I could hear the constant discussions of my cockpit watch crew.

Suddenly one said: "Something is always blinking on the ship!" Another's answer: "It's just the sun's rays hitting and reflecting from the bridge windows!"

The discussion continued in this manner, so I was intrigued and went upstairs.

From the ship I immediately recognized the light signal SHORT SHORT LONG, so "U" as in uniform. That meant the highest danger for us.

I rushed below and turned up the volume of the VHF unit. The chatter had stopped in the meantime and the French ship had already called us in English.

I answered immediately.

The captain of the ship said, "You are in imminent danger. As a French ship, we are here to make seismic measurements, and on your course we've laid a depth-charge with a detonator, which will go up shortly. "

So I raced back up, put the engine on full throttle to get out of the danger area.

We were probably only 200 to 300 meters away, when it exploded violently and a water fountain shot up into the air.

Except for a tremendous shock nothing else happened and we could continue our journey.

Conclusion: In shipping, you must always be constantly alert and on the lookout and have a great wealth of knowledge.

The Faeces Shower

We were on the 20-meter-long "Saturn" in the port of La Coruna (in northwest Spain) to take part in a regatta from this port to Plymouth in southern England across the Bay of Biscay.

I had brought along a new merchant sailor who did not know much about sailing yachts. We called him "Hombre".

In the afternoon of the day we boarded, he said he urgently needed the on-board toilet.

I showed him the door and he disappeared into the narrow cell.

Soon after, he reappeared, and I thought he seemed to be coping well.

Before we went ashore, I quickly went to the "quiet" place.

But as soon as I was in the cell, there was a loud bang and I stood in a rain of faeces and toilet paper scraps.

What happened?

The drainage from the toilet bowl was via a standard yacht toilet pump, which was secured by a valve to prevent ingress of seawater. This valve had to be opened during pumping and then closed again. In the drain pipe was a manifold and a gooseneck, the intermediate piece consisted of a thick, transparent plastic hose, which was attached to the two pipe ends, each secured with a hose clamp.

The "Hombre" had not opened the outboard valve in his ignorance and had tried to get rid of the contents of the toilet with high pressure of the pump. He had inflated the plastic hose enormously, so that the hose clamps were at their holding limit.

When I entered the cell, the two hose clamps gave way and I and the whole cell stood in a shower of faeces and scraps of paper.

Now I first had to wipe the cell clean, then shower myself, change my clothes and give the dirty things to a supply boat lying alongside asking the operator to take them to a laundry on land.

The toilet was repaired by me and the "Hombre" carefully instructed once more.

Queens-Pub Kirkwall (True Vikings)

On a trip across the North Sea on a Swan 36 "Callisto", we reached the bay and the port of Scapa Flow on the Orkney Islands via the Pentland Firth.

There was a storm and we had to stay for two days.

To occupy the time, we wanted to cross over the headland to Kirkwall, the capital of the Orkney's, to have a look around. The walk seemed quite long and we were glad when next to us an old "corrugated iron Citroen" stopped and kindly offered to give us a lift. The driver sat on a normal garden chair instead of a car seat. In the limited traffic here this was probably no problem.

We crouched in the back of the closed van.

Unfortunately, the vehicle had previously carried fishmeal. Everywhere white fish meal lay on the floor with an accompanying stench.

Arriving in Kirkwall, we realized that the harbor was full of trawlers due to the storm. The fishermen were all ashore in the Queens pub.

We joined in and got a seat at the bar.

The whole room was brimming with blond-to-red-haired guys, all of whom had hands the size of a closet lid. One of them played music the whole evening on an accordion and did not even repeat himself in his repertoire.

The drinks were very strange for us.

Relatively large glasses, half filled with whiskey, topped up with brown-ale, and a tablespoon of syrup on top.

We were all three from Hamburg and conversed in Hamburger Low German.

The "Vikings" standing next to us were puzzling over our language. One said: "Maybe irish". Another: "Maybe dutch". That came closer to the truth. I solved the mystery and said, "We are German":

Now the enthusiasm knew no bounds. In this weather with a small sailing yacht through the Pentland Firth! A very dangerous sea area, there can be tidal currents up to 12 knots in springtide and an extremely dangerous sea swell with the wind against current.

In exuberance one of them hit me on the back with his flat "paw", such that for a moment I could not breathe. After that, we were invited to another round of the same drinks, which had a similar effect.

At 11 pm the merryment was over. Curfew! The pub was emptied and everyone left.

How to get back to Scapa in our ailing state?

On an empty space stood a police car. That's when the idea came to me. I approached the two officers and addressed them.

"Good evening, gentlemen, I would like to bring you the best wishes of Mr. Sullivan, the harbor-master of Granton-Harbor. And we have a problem. How do we get back to Scapa? "

"Oh, that's not a problem. Step in. We will take you back to Scapa. "

The evening was saved. Despite the revelry with the "Vikings", thanks to the police from Kirkwall.

Welcome to Iceland

In the days when there was no GPS, Plotter, Loran, Decca or radar for yachts, also thermal clothing and modern HPX-Oilskins were not yet on the market, we made our way, with my S & S 34 "Sunrise", to sail towards Iceland and Greenland.

Our ship was tried and tested and well equipped for the time. The crew captain and the second man were trained in both navigation and seacraft and had experience in northern waters.

Sextant and radio direction finders as well as, at that time, "Consol" radio beacons were available for navigation.

Personal equipment in those days consisted of two pairs of cotton long underpants (called mealworms), a non-water repellent parka, as well as agricultural rubber boots with a corresponding "tractor profile".

The supply of fresh water was 30 litres. The same amount of diesel was also in the diesel tank for the engine.

In addition, we carried a 20-litre reserve canister of diesel. Food was almost exclusively canned. Fresh bread starts to mold quickly in the high humidity.

With the help of a few sun readings and the counting of the Consol beacons, Stavanger and Bushmills, we travelled well across the North Sea.

In the Orkney Islands, we got into dense fog, strong currents and so on, but we could clearly hear the foghorn of North Ronaldsay and safely circumnavigated the dangerous cliffs thus reaching the North Atlantic, but now had to tack into the wind, in the fog, towards Iceland.

Determining our position became an increasingly difficult task. The sun did not appear. So we added to our chart of Faroe Island a piece of paper, to get a radio beacon from "Beeren Island". Then, in the dense fog, a ferry coming from Iceland passed by us at a very close distance.

As we approached Iceland, the wind cleared, but the fog remained.

We had the beacon of Dalatangi straight ahead and the echo was very narrow.

Soon we might crash into the coastal rocks, as had happened to many a fishing trawler in the past. But suddenly the fog lifted like a stage curtain and the coast of Iceland was right in front of us.

Entering the fjord of Seydisfördur was no longer a problem.

On the way to the inner end of the fjord a boat followed constantly behind us, but it did not approach any closer, even with its outboard motor. The figure in the boat kept flapping its arms in the air. Was that customs or another official?

We had nothing to hide, so we continued on and berthed in the harbor alongside a fishing boat.

The boat was now approaching and came alongside.

The man in the boat said, "Welcome to Iceland," and invited us to his house for the evening.

First of all, we wanted to take a shower and found what we were looking for on an Icelandic fishery research vessel in the harbor, and we were provided with the latest ice news.

The first officer also invited us to visit him in Reykjavik.

The evening in the house of our "Welcome-to-Iceland" host was wonderful. At the appointed time he had picked us up with his old car. When we arrived at his house, we met his wife. She could sing very well and play the guitar. There were all sorts of pastries and in our honor a small bottle of Aquavit which cost the equivalent of 60 DM. We reciprocated with a bottle of rum.

It was a great, successful evening, which we thoroughly enjoyed.

At 2 o'clock in the morning we left the house because we wanted depart at 3 o'clock.

Our host brought us back and came on board to have a farewell beer with us.

When leaving the fjord we could see the house on the hill, in front of it stood the woman waving a bed sheet to wish us a good journey.

The further course of the journey went through the Denmark Strait to the ice shelf in front of Scoresby Sound.

Constantly wet, with storms, fog, icing, driving snow and dangerous locations, all of which took us to total exhaustion.

On the trip back we visited the first officer of the fishing research vessel who had invited us to Reykjavik, where he drove us through the landscape.

The return journey from Reykjavik across the North Atlantic to St. Kilda and on into the Irish Sea was terrible. No day under wind force 8, with gusts up to 10.

The Irish Sea and the English Channel were no longer a problem for us.

Fast Training

As a sailing instructor, I was stationed on a 48-foot yacht "Ventolera" in Mallorca in the harbor of Puerto Portals. From a sailing school based in Germany, I got the job to carry out a SKS (Sport Skipper Coastal Certificate). The training needed to be completed within one week.

A prerequisite for the course is that the participants should have already sailed 300 nautical miles.

During basic manoeuver training and the subsequent test, you would usually cover around 50 nautical miles.

In this case, however, the participants had sailed none or at most a few nautical miles. The school had told them that this training was readily available in Mallorca.

Since I am not a friend of complacent acceptance for business convenience, having had to work hard for everything all my life, I was faced with a dilemma. I did not want to accept candidates with no miles covered, but I still wanted to do the training.

So I decided that we should first sail around Mallorca, then we would have about 160-170 nautical miles in the bank.

After briefing and safety instruction, we left our home port around noon. The wind came from the eastern quarter, and so I decided to sail clockwise around the island.

As we passed through the narrows of Dragonera, the wind turned southwest and we were able to set the spinnaker. With good force five winds we swept along the west coast of Mallorca. Shortly before midnight we had reached the Cap Formentor and were now able to dash with half wind past the northern bays of Pollença and Alcudia under mainsail and Genoa to Cap de Pera.

When we reached the cap at about 3.00 am, the wind turned to the northwest, but continued to blow with full strength and so we were able to sail down the eastern coast under Spinnaker.

From Cap Blanco the wind turned back to west and we had to perform two more cross strokes. Around noon we reached our home port and had thus circumnavigated the island once in 24 hours and therefore already had 170 nautical miles in the account.

The eight trainees were knocked out after this exhausting tour and just wanted to sleep.

Since we had a lot to do to achieve 300 nautical miles and manoeuvering training in the tight time, I decided after two hours of rest to meet all eight aspirants to begin the maneouvering training.

So tie up and cast off, tack, jibe, mooring, quick stop, man-over-board in changing wind conditions.

With eight candidates it takes a lot of time, especially since it does not always go right first time.

By the time of the test on Friday, we had the necessary 300 nautical miles completed, all the manoeuvers went well and the eight participants had all passed.

At the farewell, the majority said that they now needed a week's holiday.

The same was true for me, but was not possible because I had to sail again on Monday.

Conclusion:

Without the appropriate 300 nautical miles then to complete the program within a week is almost impossible, unless you use the "whip"!

The Finger amputation

With the "El Viejo", a two-masted ketch, I was once again in the San Blas Islands off Panama.

Since I had been there several times, I was known to some of the local Kuna Indians.

As a rule, I was already expected there and the first question was frequently: "Capitan, have you brought medicine?" For this reason I always carried a stock of various ointments, tablets, bandages, as well as disinfectants and most importantly my bag with scalpels, needle holders, sutures, anatomical and surgical tweezers and arterial clamps.

Although I was not a doctor, I had received training at the German Red Cross and had been a radio operator in the Federal Border Police working with the paramedics.

The islands of El Porvenir, Nalunega, Panetup, Diatup, Chichime and the Holandesos, as well as their inhabitants, were known to me all from previous visits. Even the children were waiting for me, because I always had a plastic bag of lollypops for them.

Medically, it was usually the more simple cases. Rheumatic illnesses which could be helped with Finalgon cream, coughing, wood splinters from boat building, which I could remove and more.

When anchoring at Chichime it was different this time. An old Indian was sitting in front of his bamboo hut, he had badly injured his index and middle fingers with a machete. To cover the wounds, he had wrapped dirty rags around them. When unwinding, I found that the wounds were inflamed and rotted. Only an amputation above the finger joints would help.

That was not possible in front of the bamboo hut, and I did not have anything appropriate with me.

I told him I would bring him aboard with our dinghy the next morning.

The next morning I had everything prepared.

My instruments, and in addition a side cutter were boiled and laid out in the companionway on a clean towel.

After I picked him up, he sat in the corner of our cockpit waiting for what was coming.

To reassure him, I asked him if he would like to drink a cold beer from our fridge. He said yes and also gratefully accepted the offered cigarette.

I stood on the lower stairs, hands disinfected, and said to him, "I have to take a closer look!"

He then held his hand down to me. With lightning speed I cut the flesh around the bone with the scalpel and pushed it back. Then I shortened the bones with the side cutter, pushed back the flesh and skin and sutured it. Then everything was again thoroughly disinfected and germ-free.

All this did not happen without some shouting. But as I had held tight and worked fast, everything was soon done.

Then I supplied him with disinfectant and bandage material, as well as soap.

Later I took him ashore and told him what he should do in the next few days.

On later visits he waved to me from afar. The wounds had healed well and gangrene had not occurred.

Terrible Biscay

In 1989, I was commissioned to transfer an ELAN 43 named "Skyliner" from Gran Canaria to Hamburg.

I had four people on board with me. There were two sailing instructors, a dinghy sailing teacher from the former DDR and a retired pharmacist of 66 years who was to be our chef. I had previously sailed with him as a sailing teacher on Elba.

We sailed from Gran Canaria via Tenerife, then along the Portuguese west coast. We were caught in an easterly wind with strong gusts, but because it was offshore, it did not produce high seas and brought us quickly to La Coruna on the northwest coast of Spain.

In La Coruna we took a break, first to re-equip our ship but also because of the forecast of strong northeast winds for the Bay of Biscay which would create poor conditions to enter the English Channel.

After two days, the weather forecast promised a waning of the wind so I decided to run out at night to cross the Bay.

I had gone through the Bay several times before on commercial vessels and on yachts, even in a storm that had overwhelmed an English mine-hunter "HMS Plover" and cost it a smoke stack and lifeboat.

Although the wind still blew from the front, we made surprising progress covering almost 100 nautical miles. Then the wind increased again to storm strength and constantly changed direction by a few degrees, due to the coastline of the Bay. This resulted in huge waves crashing into each other, with huge white plumes on their tops.

Breaker after breaker pounded on our ship. We took on a lot of water!

The water penetrated constantly due to a bad seal between hull and deck shell, so that the electric bilge pump barely managed. The manual bilge pump was mounted in the cockpit beneath the steering wheel such that you could either operate the bilge or you could steer.

With the storm and the seas, steering had the highest priority.

The water in the ship continued to rise. Two men below deck were constantly trying to keep the water level low with a bucket and plastic bowl.

Suddenly, the electric bilge pump packed up, the carbon brushes on the commutator were probably too worn.

Continue to bale was now the motto. We also constructed a pump out of the bellows and hoses for the dinghy, which did not do much.

Then came another disaster.

A towering monster wave crashed over us. Blue water taller than a man struck me with such force in the back stay, that although lashed, as I surfaced out from the water I could not draw breath.

Then a cry of pain sounded from below.

What had happened?

The monster sea had smashed into the ship rolling it over onto the port side. Our 66-year-old had held onto the map table as the ship rolled over, but then had completely lost his footing, tore off the map table's boundary bar and was thrown to the lee with enormous force. He had, as we found out later later, suffered rib and kidney trauma.

That was very painful, he screamed incessantly. I was quickly replaced at the helm and first of all gave the "old man" Valoron drops for pain relief, put him in my bunk and secured him tightly with leashes.

Back at the helm, I realized that the storm had eased a bit.

But we had no current weather report. So I called all stations in the area via channel 16 in English.

An answer came from an English sea-going tug-boat, pulling a giant barge behind it.

He said his engine was at full power, but the barge could still pull him backwards at 3 knots in this weather.

Luckily, he had the BBC's latest weather report, "A low over central France and a high over Scot-land."

His comment: "When the low pressure begins to weaken, we will have a lessening of the winds. But if the low deepens, then this tremendous dance will continue. "

It was the latter which occurred and so we fought our way day and night towards the English Chan-nel. Shortly before Ouessant it became more managable and we were soon able to set the full sail.

We approached Weymouth and firstly took the 66-year-old to a doctor to have an x-ray, after which we slept throroughly due to the exertions, before continuing the journey to Hamburg.

Siren for the Sinking Ship

As captain and instructor on the Gib Sea 44.2 named "Tramontana", we anchored ourselves overnight with another yacht in a small bay behind Cap P. Ta Moscarte on Ibiza.

In a corner of the bay, acting as a warning, stood the keel of a stranded and completely destroyed sailing yacht.

As the morning dawned, suddenly unexpected gusts of wind hit us, blowing directly into the bay. Quickly a highly dangerous sea state developped, which made the ship hard to control.

The anchorage was not very good because the seabed was overgrown with seaweed.

For this reason, I decided to leave the bay immediately.

With heavily reefed sails we now tried to cover the 50 miles to Mallorca and there to the port of Puerto Andratx.

The Tramontana wind from the Pyrenees, was blowing from the north and rapidly caused a violent swell. This unstable, gusty wind suddenly abated and prompted us to reef the sails.

However, no sooner were we under full sail than the next gusts hit us.

We quickly reefed the sails down again and so it continued on towards Mallorca.

The wind and especially the gusts did not let up and so a rough, steep sea developed. This was difficult for the ship to cope with because of its length which simply did not fit the wave patterns.

The crew had put on lifejackets. I had sent some below deck because of seasickness. Two of them, a man and a woman, were on deck huddled behind the superstructure of the bridge deck. They were harnessed to the structure.

I myself was tied on behind the rudder and steered the ship.

Hour after hour passed without incident even though we were constantly had seawater washing over deck. We did not make much progress against the steep sea, but apart from seasickness of the people below deck there were no major problems.

Suddenly a huge, towering wave built up in front of us, which overran the full length of the ship with blue water.

I lost control of the ship for a moment, as I was torn away from the helm, even though I was tied on with a leash.

With loud "Peng Peng" the automatic life jackets of the crew members on the bridge deck had been inflated.

Also, a deafening shrill continuous tone started to sound, immediately drowning out any instructions.

This continuous tone was coming from the fairly large Typhon loudspeaker, used for sound signals, which was installed at a height of two and a half meters above deck on the radar mast.

Afraid, the woman cried, "Is that the siren for the sinking ship?"

Of course it was not.

Since the ghastly sound did not stop, I ordered the man named Lars to open the back box, get in and pull off the terminal lugs to cut off the power supply. It did not help, it howled deafeningly on.

Only after we had stuffed a dry towel from the bottom up into the funnel, thereby soaking up the moisture, did the terrible sound finally mute with a gurgling sound.

We continued our journey and reached the harbor at Puerto Andratx late at night and anchored there in the outer harbor.

A Hole in the North Sea (Mast Break)

With my S.&.S 34 "Sunrise" two of us, me as skipper and my oldest son, went on a trip from Hamburg across the North Sea to sail around Scotland and Ireland. We made a stopover at Helgoland, then it was north to Scotland.

The southwestern wind of magnitude 4 made us move quickly.

That night approaching the Dogger Bank, which we had on port side, the wind turned to the northwest and increased to 6 - 7 winds and accordingly the sea conditions worsened.

So fighting into the wind and against the building seas we tried to reach the English coast.

The hours ticked by, the ship pounded against the sea.

It was night.

I had just gone below deck to record the weather report from Norddeich Radio when the ship suddenly fell into a trough in the waves and hit hard down in the water after dropping 3 to 4 meters. I thought the mast must have pushed down on the keel or snapped.

The impact was so hard that our kerosene lamp, which was gimballed, suddenly swung freely overhead because its foot, which had been filled with lead pellets to keep it upright, had been torn off. The beads were scattered all over the ship.

The ship continued to pound along as before. One of the strange phenomena of seafaring.

The control of the ship initially showed nothing extraordinary.

In the morning of the following day at about 9 o'clock we met a big ferry heading towards Norway.

I contacted the ship and the watch officer said that from his height he could see the EKOFISK oil platform. From our height we could not see them, but we now knew our approximate location.

He also told us that the wind was still up.

By 1130 hrs, the wind had freshened up to wind force 8 and the sea had again become very rough.

We constantly hit our port side hard on the port bow after breaking the wave crests.

I replaced my son at the wheel and took over the steering.

My son went downstairs and dozed in a chair, always on stand-by, if anything happened.

It may have been around 1200 hrs when a loud bang startled me.

I looked at the mast and found that the starboard lower mast braces were up in the air wich meant the suppport plates on the mast bolt had to be torn under the strut on the mast.

Since the rear bracing of the mast was hydraulically tensioned, the mast immediately bent in the middle and simply broke off one meter above the loodeck superstructure.

A quickly attempted turning maneuver was unsuccessful.

Without a mast, which now hung with its sails on the port side, the ship languished terribly in the high seas.

So I dropped off, bringing the ship into the wind so it sailed under sprayhood. That was not easy, as the mast was flattened on deck, but still connected to the ship. In addition, the port side Lee supports and the two upper mast supports as well as the fore and aft mast bracing lines were still connected to both ship and mast. The lines for trimming the foresail and mainsail were also still inplace.

I shouted down to my son, "Tools on deck, the mast is down!" He did not I quite believe it, but immediately came to the deck with tools.

"Unshackle the fore and rear stay`s!" I ordered.

I myself crawled to the port side deck, sawed the three port side lateral mast support rods, and broke them off. All the time, the winches on the mast were constantly beating my head because the mast and sail went up and down in the sea.

I bled heavily, the deck turned red in places.

Now I had to saw off the trapped mast from the deck, which was not easy because the saw blade constantly jammed.

At last the deck was free of everything, but we had the whole "mess" in tow.

We tried to save something, but eventually had to ditch everything because of the sea.

Finally free, we sailed with the wind, under the sprayhood making 4 to 5 knots back towards Heligoland.

The first need was to treat the wounds.

Below deck, the rest of the mast that had come out of the mast base support had destroyed much. Everywhere were splintered wood fragments, it looked terrible.

Meanwhile, I had installed the VHF emergency antenna and was soon able to connect with the German bay lightship.

As the wind slowed down, we started up the engine and sailed first to Helgoland and later on to Wedel near Hamburg.

Subsequently, the ship had to go to the shipyard for a new mast and repairs. With that, the journey was quickly over.

The cause of the near-disaster was certainly the wave trough in the North Sea. The hard impact of the ship in this "trough" most likely tore the metal reinforcement bracing and this in a force 8 wind had led to the mast break.

Glossary of terms and geographycal regions

A black tag	A black mark on the card, to see her never again
Alicante	Port on the spanish mainland
Anchor holds	Anchor is secure in the ground
Astern	In the rear
Ayamonte	Spanish port at the border of portugal
Backstay	Standing back stay
Balaklava	Port of the peninsula of crimea
Ballen	Small port on the island of Samsö/Denmark
Ballen	Port on the denish island Samsö, Cattegat (Baltic)
Barge	Big platform for transport of big and heavy material
Beamclamp	Shelf
Bizerte	Port north of tunesia

Blue flash	Blue flashing light/water police
Bonaire	Port in northern Mallorca/Spain
Boothbay	Port in the state Maine (USA)
Bow	Bow or stem of a ship
Breakwater	Stonewalls aside in a river or entrance of a port
Broad reach	To broad reach downwind
Bucket	Bucket to draw water out the ship
Bunks	Shipsbeds
Cabo Formentor	Northcape of Mallorca
Cabo P.ta Moscarte	Northwest cape of Ibiza
Cádiz	Port on the west coast of Spain
Cagliari	Port on the south coast of Sardinia

Cap de Pera	Cape and lighthouse on the northeast coast Mallorca.
Casa Blanca	Port of Morocco, westcoast of africa
Catania	Port in Sicily
C-certificate	High sea licence all over the world
Check rope	Release the sheets
Christiansö	Small island near Bornholm/Denmark
Ciudadela	Port on Menorca (westcoast)
Clearance	Clearance inwards according to the rules
Close-hauled	In a close angle sail close to the wind
Cockpit locker	Fixed cockpit seat locker
Colon	Port in Panama, Caribean side
Companionway	Companionway steps from cockpit under deck

Compannionway	Way in the ship
Consol radio beacon	Circular radio beacon
Cross sea	Waves crossig each other, very high
Cutter naval reserve	Normal fishing cutter, grey, for exercises naval reserve
Dalatangi	Radio beacon and lighthous at the entrance of Seydisför-dur/Iceland
Damp 2000	Port in Schleswig/Holst. Baltic sea
DDR	German Democratic Republic
DECCA	Positioning system on spezial charts (hyperbole Nav.)
DGzRS	German lifboat association
Dingy	Small boat
Doggerbank	Shallow waters, English East-coast, heavy swell

Dragonera	Island and natural park southwest of Mallorca
Dröbak-Narrow	Narrow between island Dröbak and Mainland in Oslo fjord
Drop anchor	To drop the anchor
Ekofisk	Oilplatform belongs to Norway
Faro	Port on the Portugese south-coast
Feeling 1350	Shipstype, 13,50 m long
Fender	Inflatet plastic globes to secure the boat
Fire sight	Fire good in sight
Firth of Forth	Large bay in the entrance of Edinburgh
Flagofficer	Admiral of the Fleet
Free wind	Wind from behind
Full sails	All sails set
Funchal	Port and capital of the island Meidera

Gib Sea 44.2	Shipstyp 44.2 Foot = ca. 13.5 m
Gib Sea Master 48	Shipstyp 48 Foot = ca. 15 m
Gibraltar	Port in the strait of Gibraltar, Southwest Spain
Gig	Small, slim , fast rowing boat
Gimballed	Frame to adjust lamps and cookers
GPS	Global Positioning System
Granton	Port in Scotland near Edinburgh
Gybe	Ship turn`s with stern through the wind
Gybing/wearing	To be taken aback /the boat
Hailed yacht	Called yacht
Handiger	Wind drops a little bit
Harbourmaster	Harbourmaster

Hartantifouling	Toxin coloured paint against seaweed and shells
Head into Wind	Turn the ship into the wind
Heartplate	Plate in wich both lower shrouds connectet
Heave-ho	Pull up
HMS	Her Majesty Ship
Hombre	Span.: Mann
Horns-Rev	Shoal waters on the coast of Jutland (Denmark)
Hov	Danish port in Jutland
Isla de Coco	Island in the Pacific, national park belongs to Costa Rica
Islands San Blas Archipels	Porvenir, Lalunega, Panetup, Diatup, Chichime, Holandos , more islands as days in a year
Jalta	Port on the peninsula Crim
Jammerbugt	Huge bay on the northcoast of Jutland

Kaleu	Abbreviation for Lieutenant-commander
Kalmar	Island in front of Sveden
Kirkwall	Port and Capital of the Orkney Islands
Knots	Nautical measures for speed, 1 Kn = 1,852 km/an hour
Korsörnarrow	Narrow in the Great Belt (denmark)
KR	Cruiser race formel
La Coruna	Port at the northwest coast of Spain
Laboe	Small port in the bay of Kiel (Germany)
Lagos	Port at the Portugese south-coast
Lampedusa	Small island, belongs to Italy
Landing Tickets	Permit, in conection with the, C passport to go ashore

Läsö-Rende	Narrow between Jutland and isle Läsö (Denmark)
Lebet Seven	Call sign of a coastel radio station,Peninsula Crimea
Lee shore	Wind and sea to the shore
Libeccio	Southern Windname
Line abatis	Crossing a bunch of lines
Linosa	Small island close to Lampedusa (Italy)
Lisbon	Port and Capital of Portugal
Logbook	Journal of a ship
Lyngby-Radio	Coastel radio station (Denmark)
Macinaggio	Port northern Corsica
Mahon	Second largest natural harbour in the world. For 80 years controlled by England
Malaga	Spanish port in the mediteranien close to Gibraltar

Martinique	Island in the Caribean, belongs to France
Mazagon	Spanish port on the south coast (Atlantic ocean)
Mile	1 Seamile or. 1 nautical mile (NM) = 1.852 km
Mistral	Strong wind from the Rhone valley
Nauticat 52	Shipsstyp 52 Foot = ca. 16 m
Norddeich-Radio	German biggest coast radio station
North-Ronaldsay	Northerly point of the Orkney islands
Oar	Oars to pull a boat
Obermaat	Leading corporal in the Navy
Oilskin	Waterproof clothing
Öland	Island in front of Sweden, Södra Udde= southpoint
Ona	Small island in mid Norway

Ouessant	Island in northwest France
Outborder	Outboard motor
Pantalones	Span.: Trousers
Pantelleria	Italian island in front of Tunisia
Pantry	Ships kitchen
Pantry	Small ships kitchen
Pentland Firth	Narrow between Scotland and the Orkney islands
Pier	Fixed landing brige made steel or concrete
Ponton	Floating pontoon bridge
Port side	Left hand side of a ship
Porthole	Bull`s eye
Porto Santo	Small island close to Madeira
Portoferraio	Port on the island Elba
Position	Geographical point on the earth

Puerto Rico	Harbour on Gran Canaria
Puerto Soller	Port on the westcoast of Mallorca
Pull	To pull
Pump	Device that moves fluids by mechanical action
Racks	Side mounted shelfs in the ships for books
Railing	Security fence around the ship
RCC	Rescue Coordination Centre
Release chain	To give a slack to the chain
Romancatholic	Backwards with the stern to the pier
Rönne	Port on the Danish island Bornholm (Baltic sea)
Rügen Radio	German coastel radio station
S u. S 34	Sparkmann and Stephens, Yacht designer, Length: 34 Foot

Saßnitz	Port on the Island Rügen (Germany, Baltic Sea)
Sat Nav	Satellite Navigation receiver, every 4 hours a ships position
Scapa Flow	Huge bay on the Orkneys,in the history the anchorage of the royal navy
Scarph/ joint	Fixed to the boat
Scauri	Very small Port on the island Pantelleria (Italy)
Serviceboat	Small boat with outborder
Sewastopol	Naval port on the peninsula Crimea
Shackle	Connection between Anchor and chain
Sheets	Ropes between the sails and couterparts to the ship
Shrouds	Holds the mast to both sides in this case rodrigg (made of stainless steel)

Sines	Port on the westcoast of Portugal
Skagen	Port and lighthouse north of Jutland (Denmark)
Sling	Short ropes, or ends of a rope
Small slings	Short ropes to fix the Dingy
Small slings	Short ropes to fix the Dingy
Spi-hailyard	To hoist the spinnaker
Spinnaker	Parachute forsail
Spoke	To put ones´s shoulder to the wheel
Sponge bag	Bag with all washing equipment
Sprayhood	Spray guard, to put seaspray away
Spreader	Spreader at the mast, for the shrouds
Spring	A rope from the bow/stern to the miidships to the pier

Stainless	Antiruststeel
Stb.	Starboard (righthand side of the ship)
Stern pulpit	Tubes around the stern
Stop	To stop the boat/ or motor
Stroke	Old compass points, 1 point= 11 ¼ degree
Stromboli	Island and active volcano Italy
Swell	Big death sea,(bevor a lot of wind)
Tanger	Port in the street of Gibraltar (Marokko)
Tender	Armed auxiliary ship
Tholeboard	The above plank of a boat
Thwart	Seat´s in a boat
Tighten	To pull fast
Tiller	Long handle conected to the rudder

To bear off	Push off
To cleat	To make fast
To drain	Pump out the water from the ship
To luff	A sail is luffing if it is to close to the wind
To reef	To reef a sail, to make it narrow
To shackle off	To disconnect an anchor
To shoot the sun	To measure the sun angle for the ships position
To Tag	Ship turns with the bow through the wind
To yaw	Yawing, always off course
Tornados	Small wind/water tornados at sea
Tornados	Small wind/water tornados at sea
Tunö	Small island in Kattegat (Baltic) (Denmark)

Typhon	Loudspeaker for sound - signals
Utsira	Island south of Norway
Valoron	Medicine for very strong pains
Veer	To veer, or release
VHF	Very high frequency
Vilamoura	Port on the westcoast of Portugal (Atlantic)
Vorstay	Holds the mast to the front
Weymouth	Port on the south coast of England (Channel)
Wind astern	Wind from the stern

About the author

Name: Rudolf Neumann

Nickname: Lofoten-RUDI

Born: 27.12.1934 in Braunsberg / East Prussia

Grew up in Hamburg from the age of 13

Married, two sons

Jobs: Turner, Radio operator, Captain Naval officer ret. (Lieutenantcommander), Sailing Instructor A - C. Naval officer until 1988; Until age 65 sailing instructor and base manager for the German High Seas Sports Federation Hansa. (DHH). From the age of 65, Independent Skipper.

Qualifications: Journeyman's papers, Sailor's papers, AKü., Officer's Licence, SHS + C-certificate SBS-Sea, Intructor licenses A-C. All radio qualifications, including CW, u. GMDSS.

Operated in sea areas under Sail: German rivers, Baltic Sea, North Sea, Mediterranean Sea, Black Sea, Norwegian Sea, North Atlantic, Caribbean, Pacific. Total miles under sail: 260,000 NM. ; During the naval period several trips on different cargo ships.